"[An] incredible, achingly real yet enigmatic novel."
—*San Francisco Chronicle*, "Top Shelf" recommendation from Bay Area independent bookstore Copperfield's Books

"[Halfon] has succeeded in warping a modern Balkan mystery into a Holocaust memoir . . . intrinsically blend[ing] fiction with reality in a deeply visceral way." —*Rumpus*

"The most memorable new novel I have read all year—the voice pitch-perfect, the imagery indelible. What a wonderful writer." —**Norman Lebrecht**, author of *The Song of Names* and *Why Mahler?*

On *Monastery*

"A moving, reflective, and humbly resounding work of fiction. . . . As an ambassador of both worldly wonder and sublime storytelling, Eduardo Halfon's *Monastery*, despite its brevity, is truly a marvel." —**Best Translated Book Award Longlist citation**

"[The protagonist] may be the perpetual wanderer, but his meditations are focused and absorbing." —*Library Journal* **"Indie Fiction in Translation of the Year" citation**

"Offer[s] surprise and revelation at every turn."
—*Reader's Digest*

"Intelligent and authentic." —**Jewish Book Council**

"*Monastery*, which looks at Guatemala and the world from the divided perspective of a Jew and Guatemalan, [displays] a constantly surprising sensitivity, even tenderness toward both worlds. . . . In the admirable translation by Lisa Dillman and Daniel Hahn, the idiomatic, contemporary American English voice comes across as innate to this cosmopolitan narrator, without losing all its Spanishness." —*The Common*

MOURNING

MOURNING

Eduardo Halfon

Translated by Lisa Dillman
&
Daniel Hahn

BELLEVUE LITERARY PRESS
NEW YORK

First published in the United States in 2018
by Bellevue Literary Press, New York

"Mourning" was originally published in Spanish in 2017 as
Duelo by Libros del Asteroide.

"Signor Hoffman" and "Oh Ghetto My Love" were originally published in Spanish in
2015 in *Signor Hoffman* by Libros del Asteroide.

Text © 2018 by Eduardo Halfon

Translation © 2018 by Lisa Dillman and Daniel Hahn

An early version of "Signor Hoffman" was previously published
in *BOMB Magazine*.

An early version of "Oh Ghetto My Love" was previously published
in *Electric Literature*.

Library of Congress Cataloging-in-Publication Data
Names: Halfon, Eduardo. | Dillman, Lisa translator. | Hahn, Daniel translator.
Title: Mourning / Eduardo Halfon ; translated by Lisa Dillman & Daniel Hahn.
Other titles: Duelo. English
Description: First edition. | New York : Bellevue Literary Press, 2018. | Originally
published in Spanish in 2017 as Duelo by Libros del Asteroide.
Identifiers: LCCN 2017059202 (print) | LCCN 2018000057 (ebook) |
ISBN 9781942658450 (e-book) | ISBN 9781942658443 (trade pbk.)
Classification: LCC PQ7499.3.H35 (ebook) | LCC PQ7499.3.H35 D8413 2018 (print)
| DDC 868/.703 [B] --dc23
LC record available at https://lccn.loc.gov/2017059202

For information, contact:
Bellevue Literary Press
NYU School of Medicine
550 First Avenue
OBV A612
New York, NY 10016

Bellevue Literary Press would like to thank all its generous
donors—individuals and foundations—for their support.

 This publication is made possible by the New York
State Council on the Arts with the support of Governor
Andrew M. Cuomo and the New York State Legislature.

 National Endowment for the Arts arts.gov This project is supported in part
by an award from the National
Endowment for the Arts.

Book design and composition by Mulberry Tree Press, Inc.
Manufactured in the United States of America.

First Edition
1 3 5 7 9 8 6 4 2
paperback ISBN: 978-1-942658-44-3
ebook ISBN: 978-1-942658-45-0

For you, Leo,
who arrived before dawn,
with a hummingbird

I will give them an everlasting name.

—Isaiah 56: 5

MOURNING

Signor Hoffman

The sea, visible from the train window, was an infinite blue. I was still exhausted, bleary-eyed from the overnight transatlantic flight to Rome, but just looking out to sea, the Mediterranean Sea, so infinite and so blue, made me forget it all, made me forget even myself. I don't know why. I don't like going to the sea, or swimming in the sea, or walking along the seashore, much less going out in a boat. I like the sea as an image. As an idea. As a thought. As a parable for something that is both mysterious and obvious; something that promises to save us, and at the same time threatens to kill us. The sea, in short, like the woman next door, naked and dazzling in her nighttime window: from a distance.

The old train was chugging slowly down the Mediterranean coast, past Naples, past Salerno, past villages ever smaller and poorer, finally reaching Calabria. The southernmost point of the Italian peninsula. A region that is so bucolic, so mountainous, and still under the domination of one of the most powerful Mafias in the country: the 'Ndràngheta. The car was almost empty. An old lady leafed through fashion magazines. At one end a soldier or policeman was asleep. In the row in front of mine, two teenagers, perhaps a couple, were flirting and kissing and bickering loudly in Italian. She straightened up a little in her seat and turned in profile and asked him if he would please look at her nose (I couldn't see it from behind; I imagined it long and aquiline, pale and beautiful). But the boy just kissed it without a word, and then the two of them dissolved back into laughter and caresses. It took me a while to understand that on that very night they were having a big party, with all their friends, because the girl had decided to have it operated on the follow-ing day. A farewell party for her nose, I understood in Italian. The boy's kisses, I understood in Italian, were good-bye kisses.

I got off the train at Paola, a small tourist town on the coast. I was standing on the station platform, wrapping myself up against the winter cold, and try-ing to decide what to do, which direction to walk, when I felt someone behind me grab my arm. Signor Halfon? I gave a disconcerted smile when I saw his mane of blond hair, his tangled beard, his crazy eyes, but crazy like a benign sort of lunatic, the kind who's escaped from a circus and nobody minds. I'm

Fausto, he said. Benvenuto in Calabria, and he shook my hand. How was your trip? His Spanish sounded perfect, though too singsong. Everything about him reminded me of an actor from the opera buffa. He must have been about my age. It was good, I told him, but long. I'm glad, he said, scratching his beard. I was still trying to place him, to no avail. All of a sudden and without asking, he picked up my suitcase. Bene, he said. Andiamo, he said, let's go quickly, it's late, and he dragged off my suitcase, leading me by the elbow as though I were a blind man. I've got the car parked out front, he said. To take you there at once, Signor Halfon, to the concentration camp.

FAUSTO'S CAR WAS AN OLD REDDISH FIAT that only barely complied with the most minimal traffic requirements. The trunk needed a piece of rope to keep it closed. My seat belt was broken. There was no rear-view mirror (there had been one in the past, perhaps, because a rubber trace of it remained). The brakes smelled permanently of burning. I didn't understand whether it was because of some malfunction in the turn signals or in the electrical system, but each time Fausto wanted to turn, he had to stick his left hand out the window—a window that was jammed half-way: it no longer opened completely, nor closed completely. Once in a while, the engine made a strange noise, as though it were drowning, as though it were about to die, but Fausto would just give the dashboard a firm whack and the engine would jump back to life, though only barely.

This, said Fausto with a gesture at a huge church or cathedral, is the Santuario di San Francesco di Paola. Bellissimo, he said. Very famous. Many pilgrims from all over Calabria. And muttering something else, he crossed himself. I asked him whether we were going to the hotel first, to drop off my things, for me to freshen up and have a little rest. Dopo, dopo, he replied. Later. Now straight to the concentration camp, he said, where our director's waiting for you. And I thought I'd heard him say Herr Direktor, and that he might perhaps have said it with a slight German accent, and I was ready to yell at him that, while driving to a concentration camp, that's not something you ever say to a Jew.

I felt like a cigarette. I asked Fausto if he had one, if he smoked. But he ignored me, or perhaps he didn't hear me.

In the Santuario di San Francesco di Paola, he said, as we were already on our way out of the city, there is still one unexploded bomb. I wanted to open the window to get some ventilation, to air out some of the smell of dust, of vaseline, of cheap cologne, but the window, naturally, did not work. It was dropped in 1943, he said, during the bombardments from the

Allied air force, but it never exploded. Fausto acceler-
ated down a long, straight avenue, flanked by olive
trees. And there it stayed, that bomb, intact, he said,
letting go of the stick shift and raising his right hand.
His long index finger slammed into the Fiat's roof.
A real *miracolo*, he said, as though speaking from
someplace else. Or perhaps I was the one who was
someplace else, thinking about other bombs, thinking about Hiroshima, dreaming about Hiroshima,
remembering that not long ago, on a trip to Hiroshima, a Japanese girl named Aiko had taken me to
see the Fukuromachi primary school, located less
than half a kilometer from the exact spot where on
August 6, 1945, at eight-fifteen in the morning, the
atomic bomb was dropped. She and I were standing
at a black wall that ran up along the side of a flight
of stairs. It looked like an old blackboard, covered in
white markings. Aiko, whose own grandfather had
survived the bomb (he never spoke to her of this, nor
of the radiation burns on his back), told me in English
that there had been 160 teachers and students inside
the school at the moment of impact, just starting class,
and that they all died instantly. All that was left of the
original school, she told me, was the space in which
we were standing: the only part of the school that had
been built in reinforced concrete. And in the days that
immediately followed the impact, Aiko told me, this
same wall we had in front of us, already blackened

by the smoke and soot from the bomb, began to be
transformed spontaneously into a community wall,
where a few survivors from the city, using little pieces
of white chalk from the school, wrote messages for
their relatives. Just in case any of their relatives also
happened to have survived the bomb, she told me,
and came to read them. Aiko fell silent, and climbed a
couple of steps, and it occurred to me that dressed like
she was, in a skimpy plaid skirt and white socks that
were loose and bunched around her ankles, she actually looked like a schoolgirl herself, perhaps a schoolgirl from right there, from that very school. But then
I saw her put her hand under her skirt and scratch her
firm bare thigh, and I remembered that she was abso-
lutely not a schoolgirl. I looked back at the black wall.
And I just stared at all those Japanese characters in
front of me, all the white words on that black wall, all
that writing in chalk from the survivors of Hiroshima,
still alive and palpable after so many years. We both
stood in silence, as if out of respect for something.
We could hear the sounds of children playing outside. Hundreds of colored paper cranes, hanging by
a window, turned in the breeze. I didn't want to leave
or couldn't leave the school until Aiko had finished
reading me, in Japanese and English, each of the short
white stories on that smoke black wall.

Ferramonti di Tarsia, read a small yellow sign. Ex Campo di Concentramento. Fondazione. Museo Internazionale della Memoria. And above it all, like an emblem or logo of everything in the yellow sign, an elegant spiral of barbed wire.

A white-haired gentleman was standing and smoking at the entrance gate. He just watched as I got out of the old Fiat and Fausto and I walked over toward him. He looked desperate. Almost annoyed or troubled by something. All of a sudden he flung his cigarette butt toward me, perhaps at me. Herr Direktor, I presumed.

Fausto introduced us. His last name was Panebianco. That's what everyone called him: Panebianco. He was dressed as though in mourning, in a black coat over a white shirt and a black tie. He had a cap on, which was also black, Sicilian-style, called a coppola. I said pleased to meet you, and held out my hand, but Panebianco, saying something to Fausto I didn't understand, seemed not to notice it right in front of him, and just went on talking. I didn't know what to do. My hand was still out there, in midair between us, forgotten. Suddenly a girl walked over, with very short black hair, and big black eyes, and black boots, and black stockings, and a black coat, and she stopped right behind the director. His daughter, perhaps. Also in mourning, perhaps. Finally Panebianco fell silent and looked down and gave me the weakest handshake of my life. The director says you're late, Fausto told

me, as though it was my fault. He also says the people
are arriving right now. Panebianco said something else
to Fausto that I didn't understand, and I gathered then
that he must have been speaking in dialect. I knew a
little about the various dialects still used in Calabria,
dozens of dialects, some of which, in fact, were barely
comprehensible to speakers of the others. The director
says we can wait a few more minutes, Fausto told me,
so that you can see a bit of the concentration camp,
Signor Halfon, before getting started. I said yes, thank
you, that sounds good, and at once Panebianco just
turned around and disappeared through the main
entrance, limping, almost in a hurry. I thought the old
man was crazy. Then I thought he wanted me to follow him in, and I was about to do so when his daughter held out her hand, offering me a silvery pack of
Marlboros. Her fingernails were also painted black. A
fragment of a tattoo shone from the back of her wrist.
Thanks, I don't smoke, I said, taking a cigarette. Or I
don't smoke much, I said. Or I only smoke when I'm
traveling, I said. Or I only smoke as a kind of ritual,
I said. She handed me her lighter, and opened her big
gothic eyes as though disgusted, and sighing a veil of
bluish smoke toward me, whispered in perfect Spanish: Whatever you say.

———

HER NAME WAS MARINA. She wasn't Panebianco's daughter but a graduate student in history at the University of Calabria, who sometimes helped Panebianco out with the events at the Fondazione. She told me (while we were still smoking outside) that Ferramonti di Tarsia had been the largest of the fifteen concentration camps built by Mussolini in 1940. She told me (as we put our cigarettes out on the ground) that it hadn't been an extermination camp, or not exactly. She told me (as we were going in through the main entrance) that Mussolini had built it there, in the valley of the Crati River, because this was a marshy, malaria-infected region, and that the Jewish prisoners who caught malaria were simply allowed to die. She told me (as she led me toward one of the blocks) that almost four thousand Jews had been prisoners there, most of them not Italian but from other places in Europe. She told me (as we stood on the threshold of the block, looking in) that this was a model, similar to the camp's original ninety-two blocks, which no longer existed. I looked in at the shed of white walls and beautiful wooden beams, with a perfect row of fake little beds with perfectly folded sheets. What do you mean, a model? I asked. And Marina, without turning to look at me, barely opening her mouth, told me that the ninety-two original blocks had been demolished in the sixties to build the new highway across

Calabria, and that everything here—everything—was a reconstruction.

I stood in silence on the threshold, as though paralyzed, just beginning to understand that what I was seeing was no more than a replica; that they had first decided to destroy the original camp and then they had decided to build, on the same spot, a replica of that original camp; that they had, in other words, built a kind of mock-up or sample or theme park dedicated to human suffering; and that I myself, at that very moment, standing on the threshold of that fake block, was a part of the whole performance. And I don't know whether it was tiredness from the trip, or the time change, or the effects of the tobacco, or the fact I hadn't eaten all day, or the growing feeling of guilt or complicity with the whole farce, but I began to feel sick.

I'm not feeling too good, I said to Marina, smiling a little so as not to alarm her. I need to sit down, maybe drink a little water, I said with bravado, playing the hero. But she just looked at me, confused. I asked her whether she had something sweet, maybe a bit of chocolate, and this seemed to confuse her even more. I felt cold and hot. I felt my knees weaken. I was about to say to hell with my bravado and just drop to the floor on that very spot, on that fake floor of that fake camp, in the doorway to that fucking fake block, and either fall asleep or start bawling like a child. But Marina took me firmly by the arm and pushed me toward another wooden door, just a few steps away, and as we were going through, I heard her shout some words to someone in Italian, words I didn't understand but which sounded beautiful, indispensable, like the serene and precise orders of a war nurse.

INSIDE, EVERYTHING WAS DARK, COOL, SILENT. Marina led me through the darkness to the only bench, in the middle of the small room. I sat down. She remained standing, right behind me. Fausto soon arrived and handed me a bottle of chilled water. He also stood behind me. None of us spoke. I was grateful, and they knew it. I drank slowly, breathed deeply, and was starting to feel better, when suddenly the whole room lit up. There were three huge screens, at right angles—one on the wall to my left, one on the wall to my right, the other in front of me—which began simultaneously to project a short movie, in black and white, about the history of the camp and prisoners of Ferramonti di Tarsia. The voice-over was in Italian. The soundtrack playing in the background was supermarket muzak. The images were the usual ones. The bench was right in the middle of the room so that the spectator might feel surrounded by light, immersed in the sensationalism of bitterness and wretchedness and death. I closed my eyes. I tried not to pay the film any attention and just relaxed while taking small sips of water, and breathed deeply, and felt someone's hand on my shoulder, firm on my shoulder, as though taking care of me from behind. Maybe it was Marina's hand. Maybe it was Fausto's.

Panebianco was already sitting in one of the two red armchairs on the stage, holding up a microphone, telling the audience something or other about the museum. And he just went on talking as Marina pushed me down the aisle to the stage and whispered to me that I should go up and sit in the other red armchair. I was feeling better, though not completely well, and once sunk into the armchair, I smiled at the audience with something between piety and pathos.

The auditorium was full. There were people standing at the back. I struggled to understand Panebianco, perhaps because of the accent or the rhythm of his Italian, perhaps because he was speaking with the microphone right up to his lips, as though kissing it. He was saying something to the Calabrian audience about the importance of memory when Marina returned to the stage. On a small wooden table she placed another bottle of chilled water, for me, and a copy of my book translated into Italian, for Panebianco.

When they first got in touch to invite me, months

earlier, I didn't even know that concentration camps existed in Italy. My event, they told me on the phone, would form part of the week's program of events relating to Holocaust Memorial Day, celebrated annually in Italy, every January 27. They told me it commemorated January 27, 1945, the day Auschwitz was liberated. They wanted me to come to talk about my book, about my Polish grandfather, about his time in Auschwitz. They didn't tell me anything else. And I accepted the invitation because, in short, I was too much of a coward to say no.

Panebianco had already spent fifteen or twenty minutes chewing on the microphone. He was now saying something about his efforts at the Fondazione to reclaim history, to reconstruct the camp, to welcome and educate so many boys and girls from schools all over Calabria. It sounded like the speech of a politician seeking people's votes. Still talking and never letting go of the microphone, he put his other hand in his inside coat pocket and passed me a white envelope, still sealed. I could feel a wad of bills inside. My travel expenses, I assumed, which Panebianco was giving me right there on the stage, in front of our audience, as though wanting the whole audience to witness his gesture, as though he wanted official evidence of his generosity. A wad of dirty bills, I guessed. A wad of bills, I guessed, that Panebianco himself, standing at the front gate, had received from the little hands of boys and girls from all over Calabria as they entered his fake concentration camp. I put the envelope down on the wooden table, beside my book, and gulped down half a bottle of water.

At last, Panebianco stood up. He said even more loudly that he wanted, then, to give a very warm welcome to the afternoon's guest of honor. He turned to me and smiled. To the writer and professor, he said in Italian. To the Guatemalan, he said with exaggerated enthusiasm, and after leaning over toward the table and searching quickly across the jacket of my book, he shouted: Il Signor Hoffman.

And handed me the spit-soaked microphone.

MY WHOLE ROOM IN THE PENSIONE TOSCANA was upholstered in the same wine-colored velvet. Or at least with a fabric that looked like wine-colored velvet. The bedspread. The armchair. The curtains. The wallpaper, floor to ceiling.

I had been asleep on the bedspread, staring up, completely naked. No sooner had I arrived than I took a long, hot shower and collapsed onto the bed to rest a little, without getting into the sheets, without unpacking anything, and without any intention of sleeping. But my tiredness defeated me. Or perhaps the warm softness of the velvet defeated me. And immediately I began to dream about my mother. She was sitting on the bench in the small room, watching the black-and-white movie on the three screens. But the screens showed my sister, my brother, and me. Each on our own screen. Each of us in black and white and prisoner in our own concentration camp. And each of us, then, to save ourselves, had to do on our screen whatever our mother told us to do, as though our mother were the screenwriter and director of our three movies. She told my sister that in order to save herself she had to do some modern dance, like she'd done as a little girl, and my sister started dancing on her screen. She told my brother that in order to save himself he had to dig a pit in the ground with his hands, a big, deep pit, using only his hands, and my brother started scratching away in the earth on his screen. She told me from her place on the bench that in order to save myself I had to shave off my beard, that a Jew never let his beard grow as long as his father was alive, that wearing a beard was an act of disrespect toward my father, toward her, toward the Jewish people. And I, confused and sad, looking into the camera as though it were a mirror, shaved off my beard with an old straight razor.

A loud banging woke me.

For a few seconds, I didn't know where I was. I could still see or sense my mother sitting on the bench, still see my sister and brother on their screens, dancing and digging away on their screens. I ran a hand down my face, as though checking. Perhaps because of the cold, or out of modesty, I covered myself up with the velvet bedspread. I gave a sigh of relief, still half-asleep. I looked over at the digital clock on the bedside table. It was ten-fifteen at night. I'd been asleep less than an hour.

There was another knock at the door. Just a moment, I called, getting up, stretching, fighting to shake off the last black-and-white images from my dream. I found a bath towel and wrapped it round my waist. It was too small. And like that, half-naked and holding the towel precariously with one hand, I opened the door. There was Marina with her cigarettes.

Though too somber, it was the only bar in town we found open on a Sunday night. The owner, a pot-bellied, bald old man, was named Luigi. He smoked from his post behind the counter, one cigarette after another, while talking animatedly to the Sunday newscast on a television hanging from the ceiling. He was wearing a white sleeveless t-shirt, a pair of old gabardine shorts, black socks, and rubber sandals. As if he lived there and were waiting on us in the living room of his house. He had put a plate of shriveled black olives on our table, another of pickled eggplant, another with a kind of salami called soppressata, another with a spicy red pesto called sardella (made of sardines, red pepper flakes, and the tips of wild fennel, Marina told me), and a basket with slices of rustic bread. We were both drinking dark beer. We were the only two customers in the bar.

Marina had taken off her black coat. She had firm arms with smooth hazelnut-colored skin. Around her forearm she had an elegant, delicate tattoo of a Chinese dragon; the dragon's tail was wrapped around her wrist. She told me she'd learned Spanish in Alicante, where she'd lived and worked one summer. That she'd finished her graduate program but didn't know what to do next, what kind of work she wanted, and in the meantime she was helping out in a few of Calabria's museums and historical foundations, including Panebianco's. She told me that even though she'd lived in Cosenza many years, because of studying at the university, she was really from a town at the opposite end of Calabria, on the coast of the Strait of Messina, called Scilla. Like the monstrous Scylla, from Homer? I asked. And Marina smiled, maybe for the first time that day. But just as quickly she stopped smiling, as if her gothic pose didn't allow it. You're from a mythological town, then, I said, a bit haughty. Marina just took the last sip of her beer. So that's where your family's from, from Scilla? My family, she said without looking at me, has always been from there. And then she added, very seriously: Since before Homer.

At the bar, Luigi shouted something at Berlusconi's

face on the television screen. We both fell silent a moment, as though startled by Luigi's shout or by Berlusconi's face on the television screen.

My grandfather was also in a concentration camp, Marina said suddenly.

She lit a cigarette for me, then another for herself. I inhaled deeply, noticing that the end of the cigarette was damp.

He wasn't Jewish, my nonno, she said. He was an Italian soldier, she said, who was captured by the Germans in 1943, after the signing of the armistice between Italy and the Allies, and he spent the next two years as a prisoner of war in a concentration camp in Hamburg. Internati Militari Italiani, that's what they called these prisoners in Italian, she said, or Italienische Militärinternierte, in German. My grandfather, she said, was named Bacicio. Or at least that's what we called him. Il nonno Bacicio, she said, and turned to the bar to ask Luigi for two more beers. But your grandfather was saved, then? Marina waited for Luigi to arrive, put two bottles on the table, and leave. He was, yes. But he didn't like to talk about those years, she said, like your grandfather. We smoked for a bit in the white noise of the news bulletin and Luigi's mutterings. The only thing he told me, near the end of his life, said Marina, was about the day the American troops liberated them from the Hamburg concentration camp. He told me he'd never been as frightened as he was that

day, already free, walking with all the rest of the prisoners of war. He had nothing. No food, no water, no
money. Nothing. He didn't know where he was walking to. He was just walking forward, amid thousands
of other prisoners, not knowing where he was headed,
when suddenly he heard a voice behind him calling his
name. It was another Italian soldier, who was also Calabrian, called Menzaricchi. Or that was his nickname,
Menzaricchi, meaning half ear. They barely knew each
other, my nonno Bacicio told me, but the two men
embraced and wept and clasped each other's hands and
began to walk together toward Italy. Marina took a
long drink of beer. My nonno told me that the whole
way to Italy—I don't know how many days or weeks
or months heading toward Italy—the two men never
let go of each other's hands. Marina stretched out an
arm and grabbed my hand too hard, even a little clum-
sily. The whole way like this, she said with a squeeze.
And like this, hand in hand, they finally reached their
homes in Calabria.

Marina let go of me as though letting go of an
inanimate object. She leaned back in her chair, weary,
and took another drink of her beer.

They didn't see each other again for many years, she
said. But at the end of their lives, when they were both
already old and retired, they used to sit every afternoon on the same bench in front of the sea. Just being
together for a while sitting on that bench, she said,

looking out to sea. Sometimes for an hour. Sometimes not even that. Not saying a word. They no longer had anything left to say, I guess. They just wanted to be together awhile. As though at the end of their lives they once again needed each other to survive, to keep on surviving a little longer.

Marina fell silent. She was smoking as she watched the television on the ceiling. Her eyes even blacker, even bigger. The fangs of her dragon rested on the table. I made an effort not to yawn. Once again sleep was starting to overtake me, and without even realizing it I started to dream about the two soldiers in the Hamburg concentration camp; about the two soldiers walking hand in hand along alleyways and through villages and across fields of wheat or barley, battered, dirty, skinny, but forever holding hands; about the two soldiers forever on a bench looking out to sea.

Hoffman died.

It took me a few moments to understand Marina, who was stubbing her cigarette out in the glass ashtray.

Hoffman died today, Marina said again. I looked up at the television. On the small screen was a photo of the actor Philip Seymour Hoffman, unshaven, rather haggard. Suspected overdose, Marina said. They found him a few hours ago in the bathroom of his New York apartment, with a heroin needle still in his arm.

I stood and walked over toward the television set. Maybe to see it better, to better understand the voice-over of the Italian newscast. Or to confirm that what she was saying was true. I stared at the photo of Hoffman. I thought first about the one time I'd seen him in person, by chance, years earlier, in a café in Greenwich Village. He was standing in front of me, waiting his turn in line, dressed as though he'd just woken up. And I was about to say something to him, anything, maybe just hello, maybe how much I admired him and followed him as an actor, maybe how highly I thought of his ability to use his art to make a small story great, to raise to the sublime and appealing those men who were nobodies, men who were fragile and dejected and even commonplace. Wilson reading the last letter from his wife, a suicide. Jack blushing and childish as he learned to swim in a Harlem pool. Lester talking about art as guilt and longing and love dressed up as sex and sex dressed up as love. Freddie playing a single piano key in Rome. Andy broken in the car after the confrontation with his father. Phil, the nurse, administering the last drops of morphine. Scotty stealing a kiss. To tell him any of them, all of them. To tell him something. But I told him nothing, fortunately, or unfortunately. I just watched him from behind as he ordered his coffee (a quadruple espresso, I remember), paid for it and thanked the girl at the cash register, and set off again on his bicycle along the streets of Greenwich Village. And then, still seeing his lifeless face on the television screen, I immediately thought, naturally, of Panebianco. I thought with a shudder of how Panebianco had called me Hoffman by mistake a few hours earlier, perhaps at the exact same moment that Hoffman had died in his bathroom in New York. Hoffman, Panebianco had called me, while Hoffman died. As though it were more than a slip, more than a coincidence. As though in dying he had liberated his name to float freely around the world, for anyone else in the world to be able to catch it in the air, and say it, and embody it. As though the names of dead artists were butterflies. As though this was what always happened to men who, in their lives and in their art, gave voice to everyman, to all men. As though all of us men, at that exact moment, were named Hoffman.

I walked back to the table. I felt simultaneously euphoric and dejected. My sleepiness had gone. All my spirit had gone. Any sense I had of space and time and even of myself had gone. Suddenly I didn't understand what I was doing there, in Italy, in Calabria, in that dark, empty bar, in that icy winter night. I didn't understand anything.

Marina asked if I was feeling okay, if I needed a bit of fresh air. I said nothing. What could I say? How to put into words everything I was feeling? How to put into words a sensation that was so full of life, and death, and friendship, and hatred? How to find and use the right words without betraying them?

I put my hand in my coat pocket and searched there for the envelope with the travel expenses. I opened it. I took out the wad of bills and put them sharply down on the table. It was a wad of ten-euro bills, just ten-euro bills. I shouted to Luigi in Spanish to bring me two shots of gin. Due bicchieri de gin, I shouted in my bad Italian. Il suo miglior gin, I shouted, your best. Marina said nothing, did nothing. She just glared at me with violence and even a little fear. I knew—perhaps from the violence in her stare, or the olive tone of her skin, or the dragon that seemed to be biting her elbow—that she, too, liked gin. Luigi brought us the two glasses, and I handed him a ten-euro bill, and Marina and I toasted in silence. The gin was thick and strong and immediately set my whole chest ablaze. Two more, I said to Luigi in Spanish, handing him another ten-euro bill. Marina was still looking at me, as though wanting to tell me something or ask me something with just her eyes. Luigi came back quickly with another two shot glasses of gin, and again Marina and I toasted in silence. Both of us knew exactly what it was we were toasting. Or maybe we didn't. I began to feel gradually lighter.

Luigi took a cigarette from the pack of Marlboros that was on the table, and stood there in front of us. Hoffman's face, dead and haggard, was still on the television screen. The hands of the Italian soldiers were still firmly grasped together in the past, as the two men walked across a golden field of wheat or barley and arrived at the shore of the sea. Panebianco was still talking from the podium in his theme park. My mother, from her bench, was still trying to save me.

I looked up. I told Luigi in Spanish to keep bringing us gins and taking ten-euro bills. But Luigi seemed not to understand. Translate please, I said to Marina, and Marina, for the second time that day, smiled at me. Tell Luigi I want him to keep bringing gins and taking bills, I pronounced forcefully, as though giving some imperial command. Tell Luigi, I said to Marina, that I want him to keep bringing gins and taking bills until there are no more dirty bills left on the table, or until there are no more dirty bills left anywhere, or until you and I collapse drunk and naked onto the floor of the bar, or until love kills us all.

Oh Ghetto My Love

Everyone called her Madame Maroszek. A French friend, at a café in Saint-Nazaire—located inside the enormous old base used by the Nazis during the war to store U-boats—was the first person to tell me about her. He told me that, because she had no faith in technology, she didn't use a phone or e-mail, and any communication would therefore have to be by letter. He told me she liked to write long letters—full of stories and anecdotes—as well as to receive them, and she preferred that people write to her by hand. He told me I could write to her in Spanish, because she spoke it perfectly (I'd later learn she spoke more than ten languages). He told me Madame Maroszek might, just might, be able to help me find what I was looking for in Poland.

I wrote to her immediately, and thus began our slow but steady correspondence. Her letters—written in an exquisite, anachronistic, fountain-pen cursive—always came on half-letter- or quarter-letter-size paper, in various shades of white, or gray, or pale yellow, all bearing the letterhead of some hotel in Łódź. I liked to imagine her strolling the halls of her city's hotels, wandering into open rooms and stealing the sheets of stationery off of the nightstands. I received letters from her from the Grand Hotel, Andel's Hotel, Hotel Światowit, Hotel Focus, Hotel Łódzki Pałacyk, and the famous old Hotel Savoy, where I myself was staying, and in whose lobby I finally met her in person.

I knew it was her the moment she walked in. Perhaps because the whole time I'd been receiving and reading her letters, I had imagined her just like that: short and heavyset and with an air of aristocracy. But an unseemly, overelaborate aristocracy. She gave the impression of having spent hours before the mirror, putting on perfume, applying makeup, dying and styling her copper-colored hair, making sure each jewel, each earring and pearl, each ring and gold bracelet, each scarf and wrap and silk shawl were perfectly matched, until standing there in the mirror, day after day, she achieved the same image. Like an actress in the theater dressing room meticulously becoming her character, because she knows that her entire oeuvre, her entire life, depends upon it.

I am Madame Maroszek, she proclaimed, standing in the middle of the lobby, my hand clasped in hers.

VODKA AND HERRING. That's what lay between us. On the table were four small glasses of vodka, viscous and cold, and in the middle of those four glasses, blossoming up like some strange gray plant from a fifth small glass: the tails of four whole herrings, pickled or possibly raw. Wódka Żołądkowa Gorzka, the side of each glass said in black letters. Madame Maroszek raised a glass of vodka, pointed a crimson-colored fingernail to the letters, and sternly, watching or challenging me, translated into Spanish: Bitter vodka for the stomach. I, too, raised a glass. Welcome to Łódź, Eduardo, she said, her accent thick, her voice hoarse and grave. Do dna. That means down the hatch, she said. That's our custom. We toasted with only our eyes and downed the vodka in a single shot. It was more sweet than bitter, more warm than cold. Then I watched Madame Maroszek reach out a pudgy ring-covered hand, a braceleted wrist, place her glass down on the table, take a herring by the tail and hold it up in the air (its tiny body arched, its skin taut and iridescent in the bar's fluorescent lighting), tilt her head back slowly, open her mouth, and deposit the entire herring therein. She barely chewed. She barely swallowed. Or maybe she didn't chew at all and the herring—glimmering, silvery—slid down of its own accord.

Madame Maroszek opened the pack lying on the table, extracted a long, slender cigarette, and lit it. Popularne, I saw written on the pack in big red letters.

She was now eyeing me in silence: her arms crossed, her expression intense and dark and overly made-up. She was waiting, I supposed, for me to take a herring and do the same. That was the deal. That was the custom. I slightly readjusted the pink overcoat I hadn't taken off, maybe because the bar was cold or maybe because Madame Maroszek hadn't removed her huge regal fur coat, either. I reached out a hand and pinched one of the tiny tails between my thumb and index finger and felt the fish give a little leap. It's alive, I said or asked, a bit shocked. Madame Maroszek said nothing. Perhaps she didn't hear me. I tried again, and this time the herring kept still and let me take it by the tail—a wet, slimy, squishy tail. It's possible that, as I raised it to my mouth, I was hit by an ammonialike aroma. Though it's equally possible that I only imagined it. How do you say herring in Polish? I asked, trying not to look at the poor little fish still dangling before me, all stiff. Śledź, she whispered. Right. I couldn't repeat the word. I didn't know what else to ask. Didn't know what else to say. Then with a small sigh I tilted my head back and opened my mouth and let the tepid little fish drop onto my tongue and began chewing as fast as possible, while Madame Maroszek looked on incredulous as I turned green and tried my best not to spit it out onto the table and run from the bar like a child who had misbehaved. Delicious, I stammered.

IT WAS ALREADY DARK and the streets of Łódź were almost empty. The wind was blowing, icy and damp, and I had to pull my pink coat tighter around me. Madame Maroszek, standing before me, leaning on her old ebony cane, simply watched, perhaps wondering what I was doing in a coat so pink, so feminine. But all she did was take out a cigarette in the dark and light it, coughing a couple of times. She held the pack out to me. I took a cigarette. The tobacco was black and strong and made me feel a bit dizzy. But a good dizzy, a radiant dizzy, a dizzy as if from spinning around and around while staring up at a starry sky.

Walking down Piotrkowska Street, Madame Maroszek asked me how my trip had gone so far, before Łódź. I kept quiet a few seconds, pondering or recalling. I was going to tell her that in Warsaw I'd touched the bricks of the last vestige of the ghetto wall, between Sienna Street and Zlota Street, and that I had felt nothing. I was going to tell her that, also in Warsaw, I'd had to buy my ridiculous pink coat in a secondhand shop at the Centrum metro station, under Defilad Square, because the airline had lost my suitcase, and that by the time they finally brought it to my hotel, a few days later, the coat had become a part of me, and I had become a part of it, and my walk was now a Polish woman's walk. I was going to tell her that later, after much indecision, I'd taken a train to Auschwitz and, dressed in my pink coat, in my Polish woman disguise, I'd paraded through Auschwitz with all the other tourists; that I'd seen, with all the other tourists, the crematoria of Auschwitz; that I'd gone with all the other tourists into Block 11 of Auschwitz, where my grandfather had been a prisoner, and where he had met the Polish boxer, and where he had been tattooed with his number. I was going to tell her that in Auschwitz, or rather, opposite Auschwitz, while eating a very bad hamburger at a run-of-the-mill cafeteria, two teenage tourists, probably American, probably on a school trip, were groping each other under the table right in front of me with all the imprudence and indiscretion of that which is forbidden, their hands lost in each other's clothes, their faces flushed and smoldering with the blinding fire that excites for the first time. I was just about to tell Madame Maroszek something, or everything, when suddenly, still smoking, I slipped my other hand into my coat pocket and felt the white envelope.

I'd forgotten that I had it with me, in the pocket of the pink coat. I stopped and handed it to Madame Maroszek, who also stopped and accepted it and opened it in silence, the cigarette dangling from her lips, the ebony cane hanging from her wrist.

First she took out an old black-and-white photo of my grandfather: young, thin, dressed in a suit and tie, riding a bicycle down some deserted Berlin street at the end of '45, shortly after being freed from Sachsenhausen concentration camp; he's not smiling, but his expression is light. Then she took out a second photo, also black and white, old and damaged, of my grandfather's family at a photography studio in Łódź, possibly just before they got separated by the war (it's the only photo my grandfather managed to keep of his two sisters and his younger brother and his parents, and it always hung by his bed): they all look serious, concerned, almost frightened, as if they realized that this would be the last image of them together, as if they knew what was about to happen to them, and their gray faces foretold the whole tragedy. Madame Maroszek said nothing. She simply replaced both photos carefully, a trail of smoke wafting up before her face, and pulled from the envelope a small sheet of yellow paper.

EVERY TIME I TOLD MY GRANDFATHER I wanted to go to Poland, to Łódź, to the neighborhood where he was born and raised and then captured by the Gestapo in September of '39—as he and his girlfriend, Mina, and their friends, all of them nineteen years old, played dominoes on the street—my grandfather would tell me not to go. Sometimes he'd say it furiously, other times sad and perplexed, and still others he seemed to be pleading, as though wanting to protect me from something.

My grandfather arrived in Guatemala after the war,

after spending six years as a prisoner in various concentration camps, including Sachsenhausen, Neuengamme, Buna Werke, and Auschwitz, where a Polish
boxer saved his life, training him during one night to
defend himself and deliver jabs with his words. My
grandfather lived out the rest of his life in Guatemala,
and died there, still offended by his compatriots and his
mother tongue. He never returned to his native land.
He never spoke another word in Polish. The Polish, he
used to say, betrayed us.

Not long before he died, while I was having dinner with him and my grandmother for what would
turn out to be the last time, I insisted once more that
I wanted to travel to Poland. And my grandfather, by
then quite ill and weak and even delirious (he thought
his mother, Masha, was standing before him; he
thought his siblings, Rachel and Raizel and Zalman,
were speaking to him in Yiddish; he thought there
were Gestapo soldiers waiting for him in his bedroom),
shouted at me that I mustn't go, that a Jew must never
go to Poland. Then he turned to the old credenza,
pulled open the drawer, and took out a folded piece of
newspaper. Look, Eduardito, he said, showing me the
clipping that he'd kept in that drawer for years and that
he'd shown me several times already, as evidence, as a
warning. It was a page from some British newspaper,
with three large black-and-white photos. The first was
of a wall on a Łódź street, graffitied with a game of

hangman, in which the hanged man was not a man, but a Star of David. The second showed a policeman holding up a confiscated t-shirt outside the stadium of Widzew Łódź, the city's soccer team, bearing an image of crosshairs, like from a shotgun, beneath which was written: We hunt Jews here. The third showed a stand full of Poznán hooligans, who the caption said were chanting at the Łódź team: Move on, Jews, your home is at Auschwitz, back to the gas chambers. Before the war, the article explained, the population of Łódź was one-third Jewish. That is, there were two hundred fifty thousand Jews in Łódź. Fewer than ten thousand survived. But, for the rest of the Poles, what survived was their perception of the city as Jewish.

My grandfather struggled up from the table. He replaced the newspaper clipping on the credenza and walked out of the dining room, leaving me alone with my grandmother, who didn't know whether to burst into tears or try to soothe me and so instead simply took tiny sips of her tea. But my grandfather soon returned, holding a yellow slip of paper that bore a few lines of writing, in his own hand. It was the complete address of his house in Łódź: ground floor of the building on the corner of Żeromskiego Street and Persego Maja Street, number 16, close to Zielony Market, close to Poniatowski Park. One last piece of yellow paper. One last note, in his shaky old-man writing. One last testament for a grandson who receives it from his grandfather's hand, as if at that moment, at that last supper, he were receiving the whole of his inheritance.

I AWOKE WITH A HEADACHE. Maybe it was the previous night's cheap, sweet vodka. Maybe it was the bad sleep on a sagging old mattress. I had a few hours until I was due to meet Madame Maroszek down in the lobby, so I took a couple of aspirin and went back to bed and half-dozed for a while in the pale winter dawn, listening to the delicate drizzle falling on the window.

I knew very little about her. I knew her full name was Agnieszka Maroszek, and that she'd been born there, in Łódź, a few years before the war. I knew she wasn't Jewish—around her neck she wore an enormous gold cross—but that she dedicated her whole life to helping relatives of Jews from Łódź and never charged a thing. But I didn't know why. My French friend, whom she helped to find the graves of two siblings who'd died of typhoid in the Łódź ghetto, told me that, as far as he knew, Madame Maroszek's parents had been executed during the war for helping Jews, and she had dedicated her life to continuing her parents' efforts, in her parents' memory. Later, however, an old Chilean poet, whom she'd helped to recover some family property on the outskirts of the city, wrote me back and said that, from what he knew, Madame Maroszek's parents had denounced many Jews during the war, sometimes even handing them over themselves to the Gestapo at the much-feared Rote Haus, or Red House—a gorgeous redbrick building on Kościelna Street that had once been a Catholic parish house, and which the Germans converted into a police station for the Kriminalpolizei, or Kripo, and from whose seven cells could be heard the cries of Jews being tortured and murdered—and that all of Madame Maroszek's efforts, therefore, were nothing but attempts to atone for family guilt. Then I spoke to a history professor at an American university, an expert in the Holocaust years, whom Madame Maroszek had helped to find the whereabouts of her grandmother (murdered in Chełmno) and grandfather (murdered in Treblinka). She told me over the phone that, according to her research, Madame Maroszek's parents had helped Jews and also betrayed Jews; she was never able to confirm either, she said, but she had found testimonies supporting both stories. When I asked her how that was possible, that someone could simultaneously help and betray, save some and send some to be executed, she at first said she didn't know, then said she didn't, in fact, know if it was entirely true, and finally said that it didn't really surprise her, that everything in war was incoherent.

EACH AND EVERY THING about the Hotel Savoy seemed to be an anachronism. The rickety beds were

from another century, faux Rococo. The wallpaper
in the halls had a geometric light blue floral pattern
and was curling back from the ceiling. Strange noises
issued forth from the walls, the plumbing, the heat-
ers, the wooden floorboards. Inside the elevator, an
old man, who wore a black uniform and a black hat
and spoke only Polish, was always there—at any time
of day, apparently—sitting on a wooden bench. I had
to indicate my floor with fingers and gesticulations in
order to get him to push the button.

That morning, when the elevator doors opened, the
old man stood up to receive me. Dzień dobry, I said,
which means good morning in Polish, and the old man,
with all the silent formality of a gendarme, touched a
hand to his cap and gave a little nod. All that was missing was the bayonet. Lobby, I announced, pointing
down at the floor, and he immediately pressed a button
and we began to descend. Still standing beside me, he
said something in Polish that I didn't understand. He
pointed to his chest, and I saw his name stitched in gold
thread over his heart. Kaminski, I said. Mister Kaminski, yes, he whispered. Then he pointed to me and said
something else, his tone questioning. Halfon, I said, my
fist to my chest. The old man furrowed his brow and
took a hand and cupped it behind his ear. I repeated my
name, louder and slower, but he simply shook his head
and leaned in toward me, as though asking me please
to assist him. And suddenly, seeing him there, helpless

and hunched over, it struck me that it wasn't that he couldn't hear my name, but that it sounded too foreign to him, too unfamiliar, that my reality, in fact, did not mesh with his. So I banged my fist on my chest and assumed a voice that was forceful and booming and no longer my own, and said: Hoffman.

The elevator stopped and the doors opened. The old man had dropped his hand. He smiled at me, jubilant. His gaze lit up. Hoffman, he pronounced in a mix of honor and gratitude. That's right, I said on my way out. Signor Hoffman.

We were standing before six enormous graves, gaping and empty, located by the old wall surrounding the city's Jewish cemetery. A black cat watched from atop that brick wall, motionless and wary. Madame Maroszek, as dressed up and made-up as she had been the night before, told me that the Łódź ghetto was the first one the Germans established, in November of '39, and the last one they liquidated, in August of '44. It had survived so long because all of its residents were used for labor in the German war industry. After it was closed and the last Jews were deported to Chełmno and Auschwitz, the Germans selected 840 Jewish men to stay behind and clean the ghetto streets of trash, of excrement, of bodies. That group was called the Aufräumungskommando, or cleaning commando. Madame

Maroszek told me, gazing down at one of the six graves, that the Germans had also ordered those last 840 Jews to dig their own mass graves in the cemetery, so they'd be ready and waiting for them once they finished cleaning the ghetto, which they did, knowing that those six mass graves would be their own. The Germans, however, had been forced to flee Łódź before they could shoot those last 840 Jews, who were therefore saved. But their graves remain open.

We were having kreplach and red wine for lunch at the only restaurant in Łódź that still served Jewish food. It was called Anatevka, Madame Maroszek told me, the name of the fictional shtetl in the Sholem Aleichem story that was later brought to the stage, and to the world, as a musical. The walls were covered in old photos of rabbis and Jewish families and Jewish art. Menorahs adorned the tables. The waiters were in costume (I think), dressed as Orthodox Jews. A very blond and very pretty girl sat atop a small flimsy wooden scaffold, her head nearly touching the ceiling, playing a song on her violin—over and over and over—from *Fiddler on the Roof*.

Madame Maroszek took too big a bite of a kreplach and, chewing, perhaps smiling or teasing a bit, told me that another Signor Hoffmann, the German writer and composer E. T. A. Hoffmann, had lived for years in Poland, back when Poland was part of the Prussian Empire. She took a hefty swig of red wine and then, without the least bit of shame, let out a brief and charming little burp. For several years, she went on, Hoffmann was a public official in Warsaw, where it's believed he got the idea for his story about the nutcracker and the mouse king, later brought to the stage as a ballet, and to the world as a Christmas production, with music by Tchaikovsky. Madame Maroszek half-closed her eyes and pointed all around, as if to say look, just like Sholem Aleichem and this whole performance. Her hand still in the air, she said: Hoffmann was the public official in charge of naming Polish Jews.

The blond girl on the scaffold, perhaps interested in what Madame Maroszek had to say, stopped playing. I took a sip of wine, savoring both its acidity and the sudden silence of the violin.

At the end of the eighteenth century, Madame Maroszek said, after more than a century of autonomy, Poland fell under Prussian rule once more, and many Jewish families in Warsaw were obliged to officially register for the first time. Jewish peasant families, I'm talking about, who had never before used formal surnames. And that was Hoffmann's job: to name them, officially.

The blond girl on the scaffold, perhaps having lost interest, went back to playing the same piece on her violin.

Madame Maroszek took a final sip of red wine and

continued. She explained that Hoffmann, in his office, would stare for some time at a Jew before shouting the first word that came into his head, a word that a notary would then write down as his surname in an enormous register, thus naming the Jew, officially. Before he'd had dinner, on an empty stomach, Hoffmann gave Jews more serious names (like Alterman or Richter), and after dinner, when he was in a better mood, he gave them more pleasant names (like Einhorn or Dreyfus); on Fridays during Lent he chose names of fish (like Karpfen or Hechte), and on Mondays, after receiving roses at mass the day before, he chose floral names (like Nelke or Pfonstrose); sometimes, after having led his church choir, he gave the Jews names with religious undertones (like Helfgott or Himmelblau), and other times, after going out and getting drunk with Prussian colonels, he gave them military names (like Festung or Trommel). Madame Maroszek explained to me that these names, all invented by Hoffmann, became real simply by virtue of being spoken and taken down in a register, and once real, they were propagated throughout the world.

Madame Maroszek leaned forward and, humming the violin tune, poured us the rest of the wine. As we drank for a while amid the white noise of diners and glasses and Orthodox waiters and the incessant folksy violin up on the scaffold, I envisioned an entire scene in which E. T. A. Hoffmann, one lazy or ill-humoured afternoon, decided to give his own name to a bearded Jew in a shtetl, and this Jew, on receiving it, ripped off the last letter and left it on the table and stormed out, spewing insults in Yiddish. Suddenly I recalled having heard or read something about the Jewish names that, since the early nineteenth century, had undergone a forcible adjustment in German-speaking territories. The Jews' new German names were, shall we say, adapted to their Jewish identity. So, Hoffman, with one n, might be the Jewish adaptation of Hoff-mann, with two. An entire history, an entire tradition, an entire people, all in one letter. Or in the absence of one letter. I told this to Madame Maroszek, but she seemed not to attach any importance to it and simply asked me if my last name meant anything. I told her I wasn't sure, that, in fact, it was only half of the origi-nal name (the other half was chopped off by an immi-gration officer at Ellis Island, arbitrarily), but that according to my paternal grandfather, my Lebanese grandfather, Halfon came from an ancient Hebrew word or maybe an ancient Persian word meaning he who changes his life. Madame Maroszek lit a cigarette and, exhaling a cloud of smoke, smiling slightly, whis-pered: Like the engineer who becomes a writer. And I smiled back and said yes, perhaps, and finished my red wine in silence, thinking that a name, any name, is that transcendent, and arbitrary, and fictitious, and that all of us, eventually, become our own fiction.

THE BUILDING WAS A MASSIVE solid block, five stories high. The facade now looked decrepit, mildewed, all gray and ocher. Some of the windows were broken. I thought that must have been how it looked the last time my Polish grandfather saw it, in September of '39, with German troops already marching through the city, as he and his friends played one last game of dominoes out on the street, right before they were captured.

Madame Maroszek turned the handle and opened the building's front door as though entering her own house and, stepping aside, told me to go in.

I walked cautiously into the long dark hall. The yellow paint on the walls was scuffed and scratched. The floor, covered in garbage and wrappers and pieces of paper, was a block of bare cement that might once have been tiled. Madame Maroszek slammed the door behind me and I felt a stab of fear in my chest, but kept making my way slowly down the corridor in the semi-darkness. I passed the wooden doors to several apartments, all of them rotted and decaying. On my left was a staircase with an ancient wrought-iron banister; on my right an old mail hutch with a pigeonhole for each apartment. I kept walking until I reached a small black door at the end of the hall and stood motionless a few seconds. I didn't know what to do. Madame Maroszek, walking behind me, was silent. I saw that a narrow band of light was filtering through a crack in the door. I pushed the door with both hands, and immediately we were bathed in the icy white light of an inner courtyard.

I walked out toward the center of the immense courtyard and stood there, trembling a bit. The patio was irregularly shaped. Its walls, with no paint, no coating of any kind, seemed naked. Black cables dangled everywhere, climbing the walls, trailing from one rooftop to another, from one window to another, as if electricity had been an afterthought. It seemed that at any moment a little tune might blare from an ancient speaker, announcing the arrival of a troupe of Polish acrobats and trapeze artists.

Madame Maroszek hobbled toward me. She understood that although the courtyard was enormous, there was no room for words, and so she simply offered me a cigarette amid the damp and deathly silence. The smoke tasted even bitterer now. I adjusted my pink coat and turned my gaze upward, toward a dense and cloudy sky and all the small windows surrounding us. I imagined, in those windows, the emaciated black-and-white faces of so many Jews staring down at me, judging me down here. And I imagined, in those windows, the black-and-white hands of so many Jews throwing down their trash and excrement, until in the center of the courtyard a reeking mound of detritus formed around me. And I imagined the black-and-white bodies of so many Jews leaping to their deaths from the highest windows, no longer able to bear life in the ghetto, or life at all.

Suddenly I didn't want to imagine anything else. So I simply looked down, and tossed my cigarette butt to the ground and crushed it with force, almost with rage, discovering a large gray pebble beside my foot. At first I thought it didn't belong there, in an inner courtyard in Łódź, but on some sunny beach with a celestial blue sea. Then I thought that maybe it did belong there, in an inner courtyard in Łódź, like one of those stones at a Jewish cemetery left by relatives visiting the graves of their dead. Then I thought that an inner courtyard can also be a gravestone, and a whole building a mausoleum.

Crouching, I picked the large pebble off the ground and clenched it tightly in my fist, wanting to feel its cold in my fist, wanting to squash it in my fist like a plum.

THE CRIES WERE COMING through the door.

I felt a flutter in my stomach. Maybe it was fear. Maybe it was something else. I turned to Madame Maroszek in the semidarkness of the hallway and whispered that this might not be the best time. She smiled, making my cowardice clear. Then she clucked her tongue and told me to ring the bell again. This time, the cries abruptly ceased.

The door was opened by a woman, blond or strawberry blond, with pale lightly freckled skin, thirty or thirty-five years old, wearing slippers and a flannel robe. She looked like she'd just woken up. Or perhaps she was hungover. Her expression, in any case, was not friendly.

Madame Maroszek greeted her and started to say something in Polish, probably that we were sorry to bother her, that I was the grandson of a Polish Jew, a Jew from Łódź, a Jew who'd survived, a Jew who had lived there before the war, in that old apartment, with his parents and siblings, all of whom where killed by the Germans. While she listened, the woman stared at me without discretion or sorrow as I simply smiled like an idiot in my pink coat, wondering what the hell I was doing in this ancient building, in this strange city, standing before this poor woman who'd just woken up. Why had I come to Poland? Why this insistence on tracing my grandfather's footsteps? What did I think I was going to learn by visiting this apartment, which probably looked nothing like it had back in September of '39? What was I really hoping to accomplish? Was I trying to get close to my grandfather, to a tradition? To rummage through the last remaining bones and fossils of a truncated family history? I was about to interrupt Madame Maroszek and tell her that we should leave, that I no longer wanted to go inside the apartment, that I no longer wanted to bother anyone, when suddenly she took some papers from her enormous leather purse and handed them to the woman. They were photocopies from the historical archives, as she'd told me that morning, bearing the names and addresses of Jewish families in Łódź before the war, and they confirmed the address my grandfather had written on the yellow slip of paper. The woman, still standing there in the doorway, began flicking through them as if to verify the authenticity of our story, of my story. I didn't yet dare to look beyond her, into the apartment, without her permission. So instead, all I did was lower my gaze, and was surprised to see, peeking out from the folds of her flannel robe, the shy and tearful face of a little boy.

The woman looked unconvinced. She said something in Polish that sounded to me like a refusal, and handed the papers back to Madame Maroszek. There came an awkward silence. The little boy stared up at me from the flannel robe, his brow furrowed. And then Madame Maroszek said a few words in Polish, no more than five or six words, but they immediately changed the look on the woman's face. Her eyes widened and her mouth opened a bit, and she quickly stood aside, inviting us in. I turned to Madame Maroszek and asked in a whisper what magic words she'd uttered, but she simply motioned with her hand to indicate that I should hurry up and get in. And crossing the threshold of the apartment, I thought fleetingly that her five or six words might have had a threating tone, an intimidating tone. Though just as fleetingly I stopped thinking it.

Dziękuję, thank you, I said to the woman with a smile. Then I smiled at the boy, who immediately leapt from his flannel hiding place and shouted something in Polish and punched me softly on the thigh.

THE APARTMENT WAS FAR MORE MODERN than I'd imagined, and also much smaller. It took us only a few minutes to see it, guided and accompanied by the woman. Her son, a three- or four-year old blond kid, kept a few steps behind us the whole time, staring at me from afar, curious and suspicious. Perhaps plotting his next punch.

We were all standing in the living room when the woman asked in Polish about my grandfather's parents. I told her that my great-grandfather Shmuel, born in a shtetl called Chodel, near Lublin, had been a tailor there in Łódź, and while Madame Maroszek translated, I looked around the turquoise living room and tried to imagine my great-grandfather there, sitting on the horrendous turquoise sofa, a measuring tape around his neck, a felt pincushion strapped to his forearm full of needles and pins. Then I told her that my great-grandmother, Masha, had been a laundry-woman, washing clothes for people in the neighborhood, and as Madame Maroszek translated, I looked around at the fake decorations and tried to imagine hangers and clotheslines in among the plastic plants, and my great-grandmother hanging out rags, her face bleached-looking, her hands pale and wrinkled from all that washing. Then I told her that, based on Madame Maroszek's research, my great-grandparents had been deported to Auschwitz during the final liquidation of the ghetto, in August of '44, where they had both died, possibly of hunger, or possibly shot or possibly in the gas chambers.

As Madame Maroszek translated, I noticed the boy spying on us from a bedroom doorway. On the living room wall, there was an enormous gold crucifix, a long rosary, and a silk-screened image of a monk or saint. The fluttering in my stomach intensified.

The woman said something to Madame Maroszek. She wants to know, she said, translating, why you wanted to see the apartment, since it's different now, remodeled even, and it's no longer the same apartment your grandfather lived in all those years ago. I turned to look at the woman and kept silent a few seconds. For the first time I'd have to articulate an answer, any answer. I'd have to put into words something that I myself did not understand. I don't know, I whispered in Spanish as Madame Maroszek translated into Polish. I've known for years that I had to come, I said, that I had to visit my grandfather's house here in Łódź. Without really knowing why, I said. Like a pilgrimage, I said, and immediately closed my eyes in shame, envisioning myself in a billowy white tunic, with a crown of petunias on my head, and leaning on a long walking stick as I trudged barefoot through the desert. Some images, I thought, are made of lead.

The blond boy let out a shriek from afar. The woman crossed her arms, pulled her robe tighter, and smiled at me, as though embarrassed by her son's cry. Madame Maroszek started to say something in Polish, which sounded like some form of good-bye.

Would it be possible to ask her if I could use the bathroom? I asked Madame Maroszek, interrupting her. I wasn't sure if the feeling in my gut was a need to piss or simply to be alone for a few minutes, to isolate myself from everything and everyone. Madame Maroszek looked slightly surprised, and seemed not to approve, but she translated the question into Polish for the woman, who extended an arm and said something as she pointed toward the end of the hall.

IT STRUCK ME AS I CLOSED THE DOOR that perhaps I'd walked into the wrong bathroom. There were shelves full of women's perfumes and creams and lotions. Women's underwear was hanging in the shower. But I didn't care. I raised the toilet seat and tried to piss as neatly as I could, without splashing too much, and without thinking too much about the fact that it was possible that in the same spot, seventy years earlier, my grandfather had also splashed a bit.

I finished and flushed and, while washing my hands,

I looked up and discovered something in the mirror that I hadn't seen before: behind me was a small black metal locker, narrow, maybe two feet tall. The door was ajar. A tiny padlock lay on the floor. All it took was a little nudge of my knee to open it the rest of the way.

It was full of videos. Twenty, maybe thirty videos. All stacked up. All looking like they were from the eighties. And all were Polish porn flicks. I smiled, feeling slightly aroused, feeling like a detective who by chance uncovers the most promising clue, or the most unpromising clue. Suddenly I became aware of voices in the hall outside, and was about to close the small locker door, when I glimpsed, on one of the covers, a color photo of a blonde who looked very much like the woman who lived in the apartment. Except much younger, and much prettier, and much curvier. I got a little closer and began carefully to pull out other videos. Almost all of them had a photo of the same blonde on the cover, though in different poses and different clothes. On one: dressed as a nurse, cupping her tits. On another: she and another woman, in skimpy black bikinis, kissing and fondling each other in a bathtub. On another: on all fours, her whole ass aimed at the camera, her expression of ecstasy also turned to the camera. On yet another: faceup on red velvet sheets, her long legs spread wide, her hands just barely covering her crotch. But was it her? Was it the woman who lived in the apartment? The voices were getting louder out in the hall, and the boy kept shrieking, and I hurriedly picked a video, any video, either the most explicit or the most infamous or the one closest to me, and slipped it into the enormous pocket of my pink coat, telling myself that yes, maybe, it might be that in the very apartment where the Nazis had captured my grandfather there now lived a porn star, a faded porn star, and how, then, could I not masturbate later, and loudly, in Polish, in her honor?

I DON'T THINK THE CAFETERIA even had a name. It was full of old people drinking coffee and smoking desperately and we had to stand at a crowded narrow bar. The owner—or maybe she was just the waitress—was a woman in her fifties, rather unpleasant. She served us two espressos, and for me, at Madame Maroszek's insistence, a puff pastry with vanilla custard, called a karpatka. Either to perk myself up or to calm myself down, I knocked back my espresso in one swallow.

Outside, a gentle drizzle was falling. The station platforms were nearly empty. From time to time you could hear the metallic clang of an old train arriving, an old train departing.

Madame Maroszek, ebony cane dangling from her wrist, sipped her espresso daintily. I wanted to take advantage of what little time we had left together to ask her about her parents, ask her which versions of the stories about them were true. But I thought it indiscreet, and unseemly, so instead I asked her for one last Polish cigarette. She placed her huge leather purse on the bar and took out the pack of black tobacco and we smoked our last cigarettes slowly, as though in an ancient, bitter communion.

For you, she said, pulling from her purse a bundle wrapped in cream-colored manila paper, tied with an elegant white ribbon. A little farewell gift, she added. I thanked her, taking the package, surprised and also embarrassed, for it was me who should have been thanking her, me who should have been giving her gifts. Go on, open it, she ordered. I untied the ribbon and carefully removed the manila paper, revealing three books. Madame Maroszek took them from my hands.

Holding up the first one—a classic old tome, like one found in an antiquarian bookstore—she told me that after the war someone had found, in an abandoned house in the ghetto, a similar illustrated copy of that same novel, *Les Vrais Riches*, by French writer François Coppée, whose margins contained, in four languages—Polish, English, Yiddish, and Hebrew—the handwritten diary of a Jewish teenager from Łódź. His notes on life in the ghetto are extraordinary, Madame Maroszek said, but they cover only three months, from May fifth to August third of '44, which was the day he was deported to Auschwitz, where he may have died in the gas chambers. No one knows for sure. No one even knows his name.

Holding up the second book—like an accountant's ledger, new, with gold lettering on a black cover—she told me that after the war, in '61, while carrying out excavations near Auschwitz Crematorium III, workers had unearthed the diary of a Jew from Łódź, written on 342 loose sheets of paper that he himself had ripped out of an accountant's ledger very similar to that one. Each entry was written in the form of a letter that began Dear Willy, and meticulously recounted daily life in the ghetto. After having spent fifteen years underground, two-thirds of the pages were illegible, but the others had survived. No one knows the writer's name, she said. No one knows who Willy was. All that's known, from the ledger pages that survived, from the words that survived the interment and the gas, is that the writer had a wife and three daughters.

Holding up the third—a shabby little notebook with a black-and-white photo on the cover of a man surrounded by children, all of whom had a Star of David stitched onto their clothes—she told me that after the war, a Jew from the Łódź ghetto named Jo Wajsblat, an Auschwitz survivor living in Paris, had published that short book, *Le Témoin imprévu*, in which he'd compiled the songs that his friend Yankele Herszkowitz had written and sung during his time in the ghetto. Though a tailor by trade, she said, Yankele

Herszkowitz had become a famous troubadour in the ghetto. He would stand on the streets of the ghetto, she said, on a wooden box or a trash can, and for a small handout, a few coins, he'd sing his ballads and songs that used humor and nostalgia to tell of life in the ghetto, of hunger, of injustices, of suffering, of the endless deaths. (I found out later that almost thirty years after having survived the Łódź ghetto, the ovens of Auschwitz, and the concentration camp at Braunschweig, Yankele Herszkowitz, back home in Łódź, committed suicide one winter night by gassing himself.) And the thing is that Yankele Herszcowitz, Madame Maroszek said, used satire in his songs to say all the things that ghetto Jews weren't allowed to say, on pain of death, and those songs became subversive hymns of resistance in the ghetto. Everyone in the ghetto knew and sang his songs, she said, but one of his songs in particular. Geto, getunya, getokhna kokhana, went the Yiddish refrain. Ghetto, little ghetto, oh ghetto my love.

Madame Maroszek handed me back the books and brought the little cup to her mouth with a theatrical air, and it struck me that never had a gift left me as euphoric or as unnerved.

I thought I heard in the distance the whistle of an enormous black steam train, while listening to Madame Maroszek's voice as if in a dream. She was saying something about my grandfather, about my grandfather's family, about my grandfather's apartment, about the blond woman who now lived in my grandfather's apartment, but I could barely pay attention. I wanted to interrupt, to ask why she'd given me such a strange gift, ask why those three books, when suddenly I thought of all her letters, all her stories, written by hand on letterhead stationery of different sizes and colors and from different hotels, and I sensed that I was on the verge of understanding or glimpsing something. Maybe this: that what mattered to Madame Maroszek was using paper and text as a place for common ground and reconciliation. Maybe this: that what mattered to Madame Maroszek was the actual paper on which people wrote their stories, whether it be loose sheets from a ledger or letterhead stationery or a yellow slip of paper or old sheepskin parchment. Maybe this: that what mattered to Madame Maroszek wasn't whether people wrote their stories in an accounting ledger, or in the margins of a bad French novel, or on invisible music scores, or on letterhead stationery from a city's hotels; maybe what mattered to someone like Madame Maroszek wasn't where we write our stories but that we do write them. Tell them. Leave testimony. Put our whole lives into words. Even if we have to do it on loose or stolen pages. Or get up from a last supper to go find one last slip of yellow paper. Or tell it nameless or with an invented name, written down in an enormous register. Or use little pieces of white chalk on a wall black with smoke. Or do it in the margins of some other book. Or sing it while standing on a trash can. Even if we have to kneel down and dig a hole with our hands, secretly, beside a crematorium, until we're sure we can leave our stories in the world, here in the world, buried deep in the world, before we turn to ash.

Slipping the books into the huge pocket of my pink coat, and smoking in silence, I listened to the echo of a voice in Polish announcing the departure of a train, perhaps mine.

Mourning

His name was Salomón. He died when he was five years old, drowned in Lake Amatitlán. That's what they told me when I was a boy, in Guatemala. That my father's older brother, my grandparents' firstborn, who would have been my uncle Salomón, had drowned in Lake Amatitlán in an accident, when he was the same age as me, and that they'd never found his body. We used to spend every weekend at my grandparents' house on the lakeshore, and I couldn't look at that water without imagining the lifeless body of Salomón suddenly appearing. I always imagined him pale and naked, and always floating facedown by the old wooden dock. My brother and I had even invented a secret prayer, which we'd whisper on the dock—and which I can still recall—before diving into the lake. As if it were a kind of magic spell. As if to banish the ghost of the boy Salomón, in case the ghost of the boy Salomón was still swimming around. I didn't know the details of the accident, nor did I dare to ask. No one in the family talked about Salomón. No one even spoke his name.

IT WASN'T HARD TO FIND the lake house that had once belonged to my grandparents. First I drove past the same unchanged entrance to the hot springs, then the old gas pump, then the same vast coffee and cardamom plantation. I went by a series of lake houses that looked very familiar, though all or almost all of them were now abandoned. I recognized the rock—dark, huge, embedded in the side of the mountain—that as kids we thought was shaped like a flying saucer. To us, it was a flying saucer, taking off into space from the mountain near Amatitlán. I drove a bit farther along the narrow winding road that skirts the lake. I came to the curve that, according to my father, always ended up making me nauseous, making me vomit. I slowed down at another curve, a more dangerous, more pronounced one, which I recalled was the last curve. And before I could hesitate, before I could become nervous, before apprehension could make me turn around and hurry back to the city, there it was before me: the same flagstone wall, the same solid black metal gate.

I parked the sapphire-colored Saab on the side of the road, in front of the stone wall, and remained seated in the old car that had been loaned to me by a friend. It was midafternoon. The sky looked like a heavy mass, russet and dense. I rolled down the window and was hit immediately by the smell of humidity, of sulfur, of something dead or dying. I thought that what was dead or dying was the lake itself, so contaminated and putrid, so mistreated for decades, and then I thought it best to stop thinking and reached for the pack of Camels in the glove compartment. I took out a cigarette and lit it and the sweetish smoke began restoring my faith, at least a little, at least until I looked up and discovered that there before me, standing motionless in the distance on the asphalt road, was a horse. An emaciated horse. A cadaverous horse. A horse that shouldn't be there, in the middle of the road. I don't know if it had been there the whole time and I hadn't seen it, or if it had just arrived, had just manifested itself, an off-white apparition amid all the green. It was far away, but close enough that I could make out each bone of its ribs and its hips as well as a repeated spasm along its back. A rope hung from its neck. I presumed that it belonged to someone, to some peasant from that side of the lake, and that perhaps it had escaped or gotten lost. I opened the door and climbed out of the car to get a better look, and the horse immediately raised one of its front legs and began to paw the asphalt. I could hear the sound of its hoof barely scraping the asphalt. I saw it lower its head with difficulty, with too much effort, perhaps with an urge to sniff or lick the road. Then I saw it take two or three slow painful steps toward the mountain and disappear entirely into the underbrush. I tossed my cigarette at nothing in particular, with rage as much as indolence, and headed toward the black front gate.

MY LEBANESE GRANDFATHER was wandering in the backyard of his house on Avenida Reforma, beyond a swimming pool that was now disused, now empty and cracked, as he smoked a cigarette in secret. He'd recently had the first of his heart attacks and the doctors had forced him to quit smoking. We all knew he smoked in secret, out there, around the pool, but no one said anything. Perhaps no one dared. I was watching him through the window of a room right beside the pool, a room that had once served as dressing room and lounge, but which now was nothing more than a place to store boxes and coats and old furniture. My grandfather paced from one side of the small yard to the other, one hand behind his back, concealing the cigarette. He was dressed in a white button-down shirt, gray gabardine trousers and black leather slippers, and I, as ever, imagined him flying through the air in those black leather slippers. I knew that my grandfather had flown out of Beirut in 1919, when he was sixteen years old, with his mother and siblings. I knew that he'd flown first to Corsica, where his mother had died and was buried; then to France, where at Le Havre all of the siblings had boarded a steamship called the *Espagne*, headed for America; to New York, where a lazy or perhaps capricious immigration official had decided to chop our name in half, and where my grandfather also worked for several years, in Brooklyn, in a bicycle factory; to Haiti, where one of his cousins lived; to Peru, where another of his cousins lived; to Mexico, where yet another of his cousins was Pancho Villa's arms dealer. I knew that on reaching Guatemala he'd flown over the Portal del Comercio—back when a horse-drawn or mule-drawn tram still passed by the Portal del Comercio—and there opened an imported-fabric outlet called El Paje. I knew that in the sixties, after being kidnapped by guerrillas for thirty-five days, my grandfather had then flown home. And I knew that one afternoon, at the end of Avenida Petapa, my grandfather had been hit by a train, which had launched him into the air, or possibly launched him into the air, or at least for me, forever, launched him into the air.

My brother and I were lying on the floor among boxes and suitcases and old lamps and dusty sofas. We were whispering, so that my grandfather wouldn't discover us hiding there, rummaging through his things. We had been living at my grandparents' house on Avenida Reforma for several days. Soon we'd leave the country and go to the United States. My parents, after selling our house, had left us at my grandparents' and traveled to the United States to find a new house, to buy furniture, to enroll us in school, to get everything there ready for the move. A temporary move, my parents insisted, just until the whole political situation here improved. What political situation? I didn't fully understand what they meant by the whole political situation of the country, despite having become used to falling asleep to the sound of bombs and gunfire; and despite the rubble I'd seen with a friend on the land behind my grandparents' house, rubble that had been the Spanish embassy, my friend explained, after it was burned down with white phosphorus by government forces, killing thirty-seven employees and peasants who were inside; and despite the fighting between the army and some guerillas right in front of my school, in Colonia Vista Hermosa, which kept us students locked in the gym the entire day. Nor did I fully understand how it could be a temporary move if my parents had already sold and emptied our house. It was the summer of '81. I was about to turn ten years old.

As my brother struggled to open an enormous hard leather case, I timed him on the digital watch I'd been given by my grandfather a few months earlier. It was my first watch: a bulky Casio, with a large face and a black plastic band, which jiggled on my left wrist (my wrists have always been too thin). And ever since my grandfather had given it to me, I couldn't stop timing everything, and then recording and comparing these times in a small spiral notebook. How many minutes each of my father's naps lasted. How long it took my brother to brush his teeth in the morning versus before bed. How many minutes it took my mother to smoke a cigarette while talking on the phone in the living room versus while having coffee in the kitchenette. How many seconds between flashes of lightning during an approaching storm. How many seconds I could hold my breath underwater in the bathtub. How many seconds one of my goldfish could survive outside the fishbowl. Which was the faster way to get dressed before school (first underwear, then socks, then shirt, then pants, then shoes versus first socks, then underwear, then pants, then shoes, then shirt), because that way, if I figured it out, if I found the most efficient way to get dressed in the morning, I could sleep a few extra minutes. My whole world had changed with that black plastic watch. I could now measure anything, could now imagine time, capture it, even visualize it on a small digital screen. Time, I began to believe, was something real and indestructible. Everything in time took place in the form of a straight line, with a start point and an end point, and I could now locate those two points and measure the line that separated them and write the measurement down in my spiral notebook.

My brother was still attempting to open the leather case, and I, as I timed him, held in my hands a black-and-white photo of a boy in the snow. I'd found it in a box full of photos, some small, others larger, all old and the worse for wear. I showed it to my brother, who was still kicking the lock on the case, and he asked me who the boy in the photo was. I told him, examining the picture up close, that I had no idea. The boy looked too little. He didn't look happy in the snow. My brother said there was writing on the back of the photo and gave the case one final kick, and suddenly it opened. Inside was an enormous accordion, dazzling in reds and whites and blacks (so dazzling that I actually forgot to stop timing). My brother pushed the keys and the accordion made a terrible racket at precisely the moment I read what was written on the back of the photo: Salomón, New York, 1940.

From the pool, my grandfather shouted something to us in Arabic or perhaps in Hebrew, and I threw the photo on the floor and ran out of the room, wiping my hand on my shirt, and dodging my grandfather, who was still smoking in the backyard, and wondering if maybe the Salomón who had drowned in the lake was the same Salomón in the snow, in New York, in 1940.

There was no doorbell, no knocker, and so I simply rapped on the black gate with my knuckles. I waited a few minutes: nothing. I tried again, knocking harder: still nothing. There were no sounds, either. No voices. No radio. No murmurs of anyone playing or swimming in the lake. It struck me that the house that had belonged to my grandparents in the sixties might be abandoned and dilapidated as well, like so many of the lake houses, all vestiges and ruins from another time. I felt the first drops of rain on my forehead and was about to knock again, when I heard rubber sandals approaching slowly, on the other side of the gate.

Can I help you? in a soft, shy female voice. Good afternoon, I said loudly. I'm looking for Isidoro Chavajay, and I was interrupted by thunder in the distance. She didn't say anything, or perhaps she did say something and I couldn't hear it because of the thunder. Do you know where I might find him? She was silent again as two fat drops fell on my head. I waited for a pickup truck that was roaring past on the road, full of passengers, to get farther away, behind me. Do you know Don Isidoro Chavajay? I asked, hearing a dog come running up on the other side of the gate. Sure, she said. He works here.

I wasn't expecting that reply. I wasn't expecting Don Isidoro to still work here, forty years later. I'd thought that maybe the new caretaker or gardener could help me find him, locate him in town; and if not locate him, Don Isidoro himself, because he'd died or perhaps moved to another village, then at least his wife or his children. And standing at the black gate that had once been my grandparents', getting a little wet, it occurred to me that this house had had several owners, who knows how many owners since my grandparents had sold it in the late seventies, but always with Don Isidoro

there for everyone, in the service of everyone. As though
Don Isidoro, more than a man or an employee, was one
more piece of furniture, included in the price.

And is Don Isidoro here? I asked, drying my forehead and seeing the dog's snout appear under the gate.
Who is it that's looking for him? she asked. The dog
was frantically sniffing my feet, or possibly frantically
sniffing the scent of the white horse in the underbrush. Tell him that Señor Halfon is looking for him,
I said, that I'm the grandson of Señor Halfon. She
didn't say anything for a few seconds, perhaps confused, or perhaps waiting for me to provide a bit more
information, or perhaps she hadn't heard me very well.
Who do you say is looking for him? she asked again
through the front gate. The grandson of Señor Halfon, I repeated, enunciating slowly. Pardon? she asked,
her voice muffled, somewhat timid. The dog seemed
more frenzied now. It was barking and scratching the
gate with its front paws. Tell Don Isidoro, I said desperately, almost shouting or barking myself, that I am
Señor Hoffman.

There was a brief silence. Even the dog went quiet.

I'll go see if he's here, she said, and I stood motionless, anxious, simply listening to the sound of her sandals and of the rain on the mountain and of the dog
now growling at me again from under the front gate.
Sometimes I feel I can hear everything, save the sound
of my own name.

I DON'T KNOW AT WHAT POINT English replaced Spanish. I don't know if it truly replaced it, or if instead I started to wear English like some sort of gear that allowed me to enter and move freely in my new world. I was just ten years old, but I may have already understood that a language is also a diving helmet.

Days or weeks after having moved to the United States—to a suburb in South Florida called Plantation—and almost without realizing it, my siblings and I began speaking only in English. We now replied to our parents only in English, though they continued speaking to us in Spanish. We knew a bit of English before leaving Guatemala, of course, but it was a rudimentary English, an English of games and songs and children's cartoons. My new schoolteacher, Miss Pennybaker, a very young and very tall woman who ran marathons, was the first to realize how essential it was for me to appropriate my new language quickly.

On the first day of class, already in my blue-and-white private school uniform, Miss Pennybaker stood me up before the group of boys and girls and, after guiding me through the pledge of allegiance, introduced me as the new student. Then she announced to everyone that, each Monday, I was going to give a short speech on a topic that she would assign the previous Friday, and that I would prepare and practice and memorize over the weekend. I remember that, during those first months, Miss Pennybaker assigned me to give speeches on my favorite sorbet (tangerine), on my favorite singer (John Lennon), on my best friend in Guatemala (Óscar), on what I wanted to be when I grew up (cowboy, until I fell off a horse; doctor, until I fainted when I saw blood on a TV show), on one of my heroes (Thurman Munson) and one of my antiheros (Arthur Slugworth) and one of my pets (we had an enormous alligator as a pet; or rather, an enormous alligator lived in our backyard; or rather, an enormous alligator lived in the canal that ran behind our house, and some afternoons we saw it from the window, splayed out on the lawn, motionless as a statue, taking the sun; my brother, for reasons known only to him, named him Fernando).

One Friday, Miss Pennybaker asked me to prepare a speech on my grandparents and great-grandparents. That Saturday morning, then, while my brother and I were having breakfast and my father was having coffee and reading the paper at the head of the table, I asked him a few questions about his ancestors, and my father told me that both of his grandfathers had been named Salomón. Just like your brother, I blurted out, almost defending myself against that name, as though a name could be a dagger, and the distant voice of my father said yes, Salomón, just like my brother. He explained to me from the other side of the paper that his paternal grandfather, from Beirut, had been named Salomón, and that his maternal grandfather, from Aleppo, had also been named Salomón, and that that's why his older brother had been named Salomón, in honor of his two grandfathers. I fell silent for a few seconds, somewhat afraid, trying to imagine my father's face on the other side of the paper, perhaps on the other side of the universe, without knowing what to say or what to do with that name, so dangerous, so forbidden. My brother, also silent beside me, had a milk mustache. And both of us were still silent when my father's words struck like a thunderbolt or a command from the other side of the paper. The king of the Israelites, he proclaimed, and I understood that the king of the Israelites had been his brother Salomón.

That Monday, standing before my classmates, I told them in my best English that both of my father's grandparents had been named Salomón, and that my father's older brother had also been named Salomón, in honor of them, and that that boy Salomón, in addition to being my father's brother, had been king of the Israelites, but that he'd drowned in a lake in Guatemala, and that his body and his crown were still there, lost forever at the bottom of a lake in Guatemala, and all of my classmates applauded.

THE GOLDEN RATIO. That was the first thing I thought on seeing Don Isidoro's face after so many years: the golden ratio. That perfect number and spiral found in the vein structure of a tree leaf, in the shell of a snail, in the geometric structure of crystals. Don Isidoro was standing on the old wooden dock, barefoot, smiling, his teeth gray and rotten, his hair totally white, his eyes cloudy with cataracts, his face wrinkled and dark after a life in the sun, and all I could think of was that the total length of two lines (a + b) is to the longer segment (a) as the longer segment is to the shorter (b).

BRIARCLIFF.

That was the name of the camp where we spent our summer vacation in '82, after our first year of school in the United States. Each morning a girl named Robyn, with brown hair and a freckled face, would come pick us up—in her egg-yolk yellow Volkswagen van—and then bring us back at night, after a whole day of playing sports and swimming at the Miami park where Briarcliff was located. Like the other camp employees, I imagine, Robyn helped transport all the kids. My sister generally fell asleep on the way there, and my brother kept quiet, slightly embarrassed each time Robyn looked at him in the rearview mirror and told him he had the perfect smile. I, on the other hand, awoke each morning already anxious to see her, to speak to her for the fifteen or twenty minutes it took to drive to the park, and Robyn, for those fifteen or twenty minutes, with the grace and patience of a teacher, would correct my English. Eddie, she'd call me, or sometimes Little Eddie. I remember we talked almost entirely about sports, especially baseball. She told me that her favorite team was the Pirates (mine, the Yankees), and her favorite player Willie Stargell (mine, Thurman Munson). She told me that she played first base, like Stargell (and me, catcher, like Munson, until Munson died in a plane crash), on an all-women's team. She told me that soon, close by, in Fort Lauderdale, they would start filming a movie about baseball, and that she was the main actress. I wasn't sure if I'd understood properly or if maybe she was kidding me, and so I simply smiled warily. A couple of years later, however, I was surprised to see her on the movie screen at the theater, the main actress in a film, with Mimi Rogers and Harry Hamlin and a young Andy García, about a girl whose dream was to play professional baseball in the big leagues. Robyn, I read on the screen, was actually named Robyn Barto, and the movie—the only one she ever starred in—was *Blue Skies Again*.

One morning, while we Briarcliff kids were swimming in the pool and sliding down the park's huge slide, a man drowned.

I remember the adults shouting, telling us all to get out of the water, then the younger kids crying, then the sirens of the ambulance, then the lifeless body of the man laid out beside the small maintenance pool where he'd drowned, two or three paramedics around him, trying to resuscitate him. I was somewhat far from the scene, still wet and in my bathing suit, but for a few instants, through the paramedics' legs, I could make out the blue-tinged face of the man on the ground. A pale blue, washed-out, between indigo and azure. A blue I'd never seen before. A blue that shouldn't exist in the pantone of blues. And seeing the man on the ground, I immediately pictured Salomón floating in the lake, Salomón faceup in the lake, his face now forever tinged the same shade of blue.

That night, on the way home in the Volkswagen van, I waited until my brother and sister were asleep to ask Robyn what had happened to the man. She kept quiet for a good while, just driving in the dark of the night, and I thought that she hadn't heard me or that perhaps she didn't want to talk about it. But eventually she told me in a hushed tone that the man had gotten trapped underwater in the small maintenance pool. That the man's right arm had gotten caught, she told me, while he was cleaning the filter for the slide. That the man had died, she told me, without anyone seeing.

WHEN WE WERE KIDS, we believed Don Isidoro when he told us that what he was drinking from a small metal canteen—which smelled like pure alcohol—was his medicine. And we believed him when he told us that the rumblings of hunger our tummies made were the hisses of an enormous black snake slithering around in there, and that it went in and out through our belly buttons while we slept. And we believed him when he told us that the ever more frequent gunfire and bomb blasts in the mountains were only eruptions of the Pacaya volcano. And we believed him when he told us that the two bodies that turned up one morning floating by the dock were not two murdered guerillas tossed into the lake, but two normal boys, two boys scuba diving. And we believed him when he told us that, if we didn't behave, at night a sorceress would come for us, a sorceress who lived in a cave at the bottom of the lake (my brother—I don't know if by mistake or as a joke—called her the Shore-ceress of the Lake), a dark cave where she waited for all the spoiled little white boys and girls she stole from the lake houses.

WHEN WE WERE KIDS, we used to help Don Isidoro plant trees around the property. Don Isidoro would open up a hole with a pickax and then move to one side and allow us to put in the sapling and then fill the hole back up with black earth. I remember that we planted a eucalyptus by the gate, a row of cypresses along the line bordering our neighbor's land, a small matilisguate by the lakeshore. I remember Don Isidoro telling us that, before we filled each hole with earth, we had to bring our heads in close and whisper a word of encouragement into the hole, a pretty word, a word that would help the tree take root and grow properly (my brother, invariably, whispered good-bye). The word, Don Isidoro told us, would remain there forever, buried in the black earth.

When we were kids, Don Isidoro would often take us out for a ride around the lake, the three of us sitting on a long surfboard, straddling it, feet in the water. When we got far enough from the house, and despite Don Isidoro's threats, my brother and I would remove the uncomfortable orange life vests and threaten to toss them away (on one of those trips, perhaps the last one we made, as I was timing how long it took from the start point to the end point, the black plastic watch slipped off my too-thin wrist, fell into the water and disappeared into the lake). For balance, I suppose, Don Isidoro always sat in the center of the board, between us. My brother always sat at the tip, and from the tip he'd say that he was captain and give Don Isidoro orders about where to row. From time to time, little black fish would break through the lake's surface and land on the acrylic board and we had to nudge them gently back into the water.

WHEN WE WERE KIDS, Don Isidoro told us that the word Amatitlán, in the language of his ancestors, means place surrounded by amates, which are huge ficus trees, due to all the amate trees around the lake. Other times he told us that the word Amatitlán, in the language of his ancestors, means city of letters, due to the glyphs his ancestors cut into the trunks of the trees by the lake. Still other times, laughing, he told us that the word Amatitlán doesn't mean anything anymore.

WHEN WE WERE KIDS, Don Isidoro used to take us to a secret beach on the lake. We'd walk out through the black gate and down the road with him—my brother holding one hand, I the other—until we got to a narrow path, hardly visible, thick with branches and shrubs, that finally ended at a muddy beach on the lake. Don Isidoro would tell us it was a secret beach. He would tell us we must never reveal it to anyone. And then, after we had sat down in the mud, Don Isidoro would take off his shirt, walk slowly into the water, and disappear entirely. We'd remain onshore, waiting, well behaved in the mud, always fearing that Don Isidoro wouldn't reappear (my brother, without fail, would cry). But Don Isidoro always reappeared. He always emerged from the water all brown and radiant and always carrying some mysterious clay object. We were too young to understand that Don Isidoro was removing Mayan archaeological pieces from the lake bed, pre-Columbian pots and jugs, perhaps made by his own ancestors, which he would then sell to one of my uncles for a few dollars.

WHEN WE WERE KIDS, Don Isidoro sometimes led us to a back patio behind my grandparents' house, a dark narrow patio full of laundry hung out to dry, and once back there, tucked away on that patio, he taught us to kneel, to cross ourselves, to pray like two good Catholic boys. Then, as we prayed in confusion and my brother held tight to my arm, Don Isidoro would whisper to us that maybe this way the Lord would forgive us the sin of having killed His son.

I WAS DYING OF HUNGER. Sitting between my two grandfathers, the Polish one and the Lebanese one, I was dying of hunger. They had traveled up from Guatemala to spend the Jewish holidays with us. It was late afternoon and Plantation's synagogue was full. Kol Ami, the synagogue was called: voice of my people, in Hebrew. It was hot. I was thirteen years old and only a couple of hours from finishing my first complete fast on Yom Kippur, the day of atonement, of forgiveness, of repentance, when Jews fast for twenty-five hours, from sundown to sundown.

No food. No water. My mother was sitting with my sister and my grandmothers and the other women. My brother was sitting with my father, far from me, a few rows behind us. He was not yet thirteen, he was still a boy, he had already eaten. But more than hunger, I remember the thirst. And the stink of some of the old men (my father explained to me that, for fear of swallowing a few drops of water, they didn't bathe, either). And the feeling that it was all theater: the men around me talking business, making jokes, asking me if I had a girlfriend yet. But what I remember most is that I spent the entire prayer looking up, making little attempt to hide that I was staring at the mouth of my maternal grandfather, my Polish grandfather. That morning, with all of us already rushing to leave for synagogue, I had come upon him sitting on the bed in the guest room, still in his pajamas. My grandfather had quickly covered his mouth with one hand and stammered something in Spanish as in horror I spotted the false teeth beside him, on the nightstand, all pink and shiny in a glass of water. It had never occurred to me that on his arrival in Guatemala in 1946, when he was barely twenty-five years old, after the war, after being prisoner in several concentration camps, my Polish grandfather had already lost all of his teeth.

A few days before Yom Kippur, my Polish grandfather had taken my brother and me to a hangar full of old airplanes in Miami.

He was strangely fascinated by airplanes. Several times I'd found him in front of the television, the volume up too loud, completely absorbed in some old documentary or report on the history of aviation. As a very young boy, in Guatemala, I often accompanied my grandfather on his walks around the neighborhood, and he always liked to pass the empty field where one night a cargo plane full of cows had crashed. That image, of a plane full of cows falling from the sky in the middle of the city, captivated me my entire childhood. Sometimes I imagined the cows sitting primly in their seats. Other times I imagined them floating in an enormous empty plane. Other times wandering down the long aisle of a plane with pails of hay on the floor. Today, of course, I know that my imagination latched onto a mistake, and that the reality was different: the owner of that empty field kept a herd of cows there, grazing, and they had all been killed when one night a cargo plane fell on them.

Wings Over Miami, that was the name of the hangar. It was a kind of museum of aviation, my grandfather told us. Neither my brother nor I wanted to go. We didn't like museums, or airplanes, much less the history of airplanes, and the mere idea of having to spend an entire afternoon with our grandfather, looking at relics of the history of aviation, already had us wavering between boredom and dread. But my grandfather, who rarely insisted, insisted.

I remember little about that afternoon, except that we drove around Miami for hours looking for the hangar, and that then we walked in circles around the hangar itself, following my grandfather through the museum at a distance as he attempted to find I don't know what plane. Finally, a museum employee took pity on him and led us to a warplane—huge, all rusty and gray, suspended from the ceiling. My grandfather gazed up at it for a long time, I couldn't say exactly how long, but I remember it as interminable. He didn't say anything. He had no expression on his face. No euphoria or satisfaction at having found the plane he'd been looking for, and which was obviously the reason why we were there. Then my grandfather looked down and told us that that was all, that we could leave now, and so we left, and it would not be until thirty years later, on a trip to Berlin, that I finally understood, or thought I understood, the lack of expression on his face, and perhaps also the significance for my grandfather of that afternoon in the airplane museum.

I was in Berlin for only a few days, on my way to Poland, to Łódź, and a friend offered to go with me to visit Sachsenhausen, one of the concentration camps where my grandfather had been a prisoner during the war. But I told her that I didn't want to or that I couldn't or maybe that I wasn't interested. I had already seen too much in Germany. I didn't want to see or remember any more.

Before Berlin, I'd been in Cologne for a few days, to give a talk at the university, and all over the city I began discovering small bronze plaques: plaques and plaques and more bronze plaques in the ground, stuck between the actual cobblestones of the sidewalk, each ten centimeters by ten centimeters and engraved with the name and date of the Jew who had lived there, in that house in Cologne, before being captured and murdered by the Nazis. Like little bronze gravestones, it struck me, for all the Jews of Cologne who'd died never having had a proper gravestone, a dignified gravestone. Stolperstein, these plaques are called, they told me at the university. The word in German means something like stumble stone, they explained. The origin of the name, they explained, at least in part, comes from an old expression Germans often used when they stumbled in the street: Hier könnte ein Jude begraben sein. A Jew could be buried here.

And before Berlin, I had also been in Frankfurt for a few days, also invited to give a talk at the university, on the central campus of Goethe University: an immense, beautiful building erected in 1930 as the headquarters of IG Farben, at the time the largest chemical company in the world, they explained to me at the university, and the principal manufacturer of Zyklon B gas for the Nazis (prior to the building's construction in 1930, they explained, there had been an insane asylum there, whose director was another Hoffman, the doctor and writer Heinrich Hoffmann, a fact that struck me as historically logical). IG Farben, originally specializing in the eradication of plagues of insects, they explained, became a cartel controlled by the Third Reich, and their pesticides were diverted for the extermination of what they considered a greater plague. And as I gave my talk in an old and ostentatious hall, I couldn't stop thinking that right there, in that same building that was now a great university, they had developed and produced the cylinders of gas that killed my grandfather's sisters, my grandfather's parents.

I tried to tell my friend in Berlin that I'd already seen too much on my travels around Germany, that I was starting to lose the scope of the tragedy, that I wasn't interested in visiting concentration camps, not even one of those where my grandfather had been a prisoner, that to me every concentration camp was nothing but a tourist attraction dedicated to profiting from human suffering. But finally I gave in. In part because I'm weak and find it hard to say no to women. In part because that entire trip was a sort of tribute to my Polish grandfather, who had arrived in Guatemala after surviving for six years—the entire war—as a prisoner in concentration camps. When I was a boy I knew almost nothing about his experience during the war beyond the fact that some German or Polish soldiers had captured him in front of his family apartment in Łódź, in November of 1939, when he was twenty years old, while he was playing dominoes with some friends and cousins. My grandfather never spoke to me of those six years, or of the camps, or of the deaths of his siblings and parents. I had to go about discovering the details little by little, in his gestures and in his jokes and almost in spite of him. When I was a boy, if I left food on my plate, my grandfather, rather than scolding me or saying anything to me, would simply reach a hand out in silence and finish all the food himself. When I was a boy, my grandfather told me that the numbered tattooed on his left forearm (69752) was his telephone number, and that he'd tattooed it there so he wouldn't forget it. And as a boy, of course, I believed him.

The following morning, we boarded a train which, in under an hour, left us at the station in a town called Oranienburg, and from there an ill-tempered taxi driver took us to the black-gated entrance of the concentration camp. That simple, that fast.

The day was cool and cloudy and I kept looking not at the concentration camp before me, but at the old residential neighborhood just across the street. A girl of three or four was riding a red tricycle. An older woman with yellow gloves was crouched down, pottering around a rosebush. A couple of teenagers were walking down the sidewalk, holding hands and giving each other little kisses. And it occurred to me that this—a girl playing, an older woman pruning her rosebushes, a couple falling in love—was exactly how the neighborhood must have looked seventy years ago, during the war. I have always been more appalled by man's apathy in the face of horror than by the horror itself.

We toured the camp quickly, walking its entire perimeter, which was originally shaped, I realized in amazement, like an equilateral triangle. My friend was trying to show or explain a few things to me, and I was just begging her for us to keep going. The truth is that I didn't want to know anything about that place, didn't want to be there; all I wanted was to pick up the pace and finish the visit as soon as possible and go have a beer at some tavern in town. But my friend just kept walking along with the other tourists. We saw the old prisoners' barracks. The director's house, the infirmary, the watchtowers. A torture device known as the Rack, perhaps exactly the same one on which my grandfather, after being caught with a twenty-dollar gold coin, received I don't know how many blows to the coccyx with a wooden or iron rod, until he lost consciousness. We saw Station Z, an area built for the purpose of murdering prisoners, comprised of four crematoria, several rooms where they were killed with a shot to the back of the head, and a gas chamber;

its name, rather mockingly, referred to the last letter of the alphabet. Upon finishing the tour, my friend and I entered the museum's reception area. There was a cafeteria, a small shop. My friend asked me if I wanted to get anything to eat or to buy anything, and as I was about to say no, how was I going to want to eat or buy anything at a concentration camp, I discovered a glass door at the end of the hall that seemed to be somebody's office, or the administration office. I asked my friend what it was and she read me the sign painted on the glass. Archiv Gedenkstätte und Museum Sachsenhausen, she told me. The Sachsenhausen Museum and Memorial Archive. I asked her if it was possible that they had any information there about my grandfather, about the time he'd spent in Sachsenhausen, and my friend, smiling now, began walking toward the glass door.

We spent two or three hours searching through the old books and papers (they still had nothing digitized) for any information about my grandfather, León Tenenbaum. A young woman, pale, her head shaved, a ring in her nose and wearing a white lab coat, seated us at an enormous table and brought us books and records, all dusty, all original, all in the type or actual handwriting of some German official. It didn't help that I didn't know the precise dates my grandfather had been prisoner there. He himself didn't know, or didn't remember, or had never told me. The girl explained to us in German—which my friend translated for me into Spanish—that practically all of the documents from the concentration camp's command headquarters, including the registration cards and almost all of the records relating to them, had been destroyed by the SS in the spring of 1945, in light of the camp's imminent liberation; and that the few documents that had been preserved were now incomplete and dispersed through several books and archives, especially Soviet archives. Our task suddenly struck me as futile. I was about to close everything and give up, when the girl asked me something in German, which my friend immediately translated. Are you sure your grandfather didn't have another name? At first I didn't understand the question, nor did I give it much importance. But then it occurred to me that León was the Spanish version of his name, and I remembered that my grandmother never called him León, but used his Yiddish name, Leib. And that's what I told my friend, and that's what she translated to the lab girl, and that's how easily the final lock was unlocked, and in we went.

My grandfather, Leib Tenenbaum, not León Tenenbaum, first prisoner number 9860, then prisoner number 13664, had been in Sachsenhausen until his transfer, on November 19, 1939, to the concentration camp at Neuengamme, near Hamburg, where he became prisoner number 131333. A little more than five years later, on February 13, 1945, now as prisoner number 69752 (the number he received and was tattooed with in Auschwitz), he'd returned once more to Sachsenhausen, but this time they'd placed him in the Arbeitslager Heinkel, the Heinkel forced labor camp.

I didn't understand the jumble of numbers. Why so many numbers? Why keep changing the numbers? As though in war a prisoner were, in fact, many prisoners, and a man many men. What's more, I knew about his time in Neuengamme and then Auschwitz, where they tattooed the number on his left forearm and where a Polish boxer who was also from Łódź saved his life, but this was the first time I'd heard the name Heinkel. I asked my friend what this Heinkel business was, and she and the lab girl spoke for a time in German. Heinkel, my friend finally explained to me, was a factory near there, in Oranienburg, where the Nazis manufactured warplanes, one model in particular, the He 177. Your grandfather worked there, at Heinkel, she said, during the final months of the war. I told her that it wasn't possible, that my grandfather had never even mentioned the place. The lab girl, as though she'd understood my skepticism, pointed her index finger to the dusty yellowed page of the record book. Der Beweis, she said in German. The evidence, she said in English. Then she began to tell a story in German to my friend, and I had to wait a few minutes for my friend to translate it into Spanish.

The Heinkel He 177 warplane was a heavy bomber with long-range capability. In the final months of the war, several of these planes fell near Stalingrad, mysteriously, without having clashed with Allied planes, without anyone understanding why. And no one ever found out why. It is believed, my friend told me, to have been an act of sabotage on the part of some of the Jewish prisoners forced to work in the Heinkel factory in Oranienburg. It is believed, she told me, that some Jews in Oranienburg, in their own way, helped bring down a fleet of Nazi warplanes. It's possible, my friend told me, that your grandfather was one of those Jews.

My Polish grandfather's younger brother, his only brother, the one who would have been my Polish great-uncle had he not died in the war, was also named Salomón. Or rather, he was named Zalman, which is Salomón in Yiddish. We have, in the family, just one remaining photo of him, that's it, a single photo as proof of his existence, of the fact that one such Zalman ever existed. It's an old and damaged image of the six members of my grandfather's family, likely taken in a photography studio in Łódź just before the war broke out, and which my grandfather, for the rest of his life, would hang by his bed, above the nightstand. Sometimes my grandfather said he'd gotten the photo from one of his uncles who left Poland before '39. Other times he said that he

himself had managed to hold on to it through the six
years he spent in the camps, carefully hidden who knows
where, and then bring it with him to Guatemala. The
young Zalman, in the photo, looks frightened, almost
sad, as though he knew the fate awaiting him. My grandfather always told me that his younger brother was the
kinder one, the better student, and that he'd died during
the war. But he never told me how he'd died, or where, or
why, perhaps because he himself didn't know (as a boy, I
often looked at that old photo on the wall by his bed and
imagined that my grandfather's younger brother, like all
Salomón boys, had also drowned in a lake). No one in
the family knew the details of his death. Maybe nobody
wanted to know them.

A few years back, I finally took a trip to Łódź.

I stayed at the famous and antiquated Hotel Savoy,
while reading the homonymous Joseph Roth novel and
befriending the elevator operator, an old man in a black
uniform and black cap with the surname Kaminski,
or at least with the surname Kaminski embroidered
in gold on his chest, and who seemed always to be in
the elevator, sitting and waiting at all times on his little
wooden bench. Whenever he saw me enter, old Kaminski would stand, make a slight gesture of reverence with
his cap, say dzień dobry, Mister Hoffman, and then,
pounding one fist to his chest, begin speaking to me in
Polish as though I understood, and I'd respond to him
in Spanish as though he understood.

My grandfather never went back to his native city. He never wanted to go back. Nor did he allow anyone in the family to go. You must not go to Poland, he said. The Poles, he would say again and again, betrayed us. I traveled to Poland against his wishes, then, but with a small yellow slip of paper on which he himself had written, shortly before his death, the exact address of his house in Łódź, the full names of his parents and siblings. A final order or decree, perhaps, or perhaps a kind of trepverter, as my grandfather would have called it, which in Yiddish means words we should have said but come to us after it's already too late, when we're already walking down the stairs, already on the way out.

In one of the many old record books kept in the office of the city's Jewish community center, and with the help of Madame Maroszek, we at last came upon a delicate, faded document, all typed out in Polish and with registration number 1613, that explained how Zalman had died in the ghetto in Łódź, at number 12 Rauch Street (now Wolborska Street, Madame Maroszek explained), on June 14, 1944, a few months before the liquidation of the ghetto. My grandfather's younger brother, said the document, barely twenty years old, had died of hunger.

I WAS STILL HUNGRY, still looking up at my grandfather's false teeth, when the rabbi at the Plantation synagogue stopped right in front of me. He was a handsome man, with dark skin and green eyes. He looked like he was boiling in his long white satin robe. He was holding a thin silver rod whose tip was a miniature hand, its index finger extended, pointing. My two grandfathers stood.

The rabbi said something to them gravely, his face bathed in sweat. I didn't know if I should stand as well, so I remained seated, looking up at them, hearing how my grandfathers began whispering names and numbers to the rabbi. One of my grandfathers would say a name and the rabbi would repeat that name and then my grand-father would say a number and the rabbi would repeat that number. And on like that. Names and numbers. One of my grandfathers, then the other. And the rabbi was taking note of it all. Masha, whispered my Polish grandfather, and then he said a number. Myriam, whis-pered my Lebanese grandfather, and then said another number. Shmuel, whispered my Polish grandfather, and then said another number. Bela, whispered my Leba-nese grandfather, and then said another number. I was a little frightened. I understood nothing. Perhaps because of my grandfathers' whispering, it all seemed part of a secret or forbidden ceremony. I turned and was about to ask my father what was going on, but he shouted at me with his eyes and so I thought bet-ter of it and kept quiet. My grandparents continued standing, continued whispering names and numbers, and more names and numbers, and then, amid all that whispering, I clearly heard my Lebanese grandfather pronounce the name Salomón.

The prayer finally ended. We all went out into the lobby, where there was a long table with crackers and cookies and orange juice and coffee, to break the fast. The kids, no longer in jackets and ties, were running all over. The adults were hardly speaking. My father told me to eat slowly, to eat very little. I had a powdery cookie in my hand and was taking small bites when I asked my father in English why my grandfathers had told the rabbi all those names. With some trouble, my father explained to me in Spanish that that was the prayer to honor the memory of the dead. Yizkor, it's called, he said. And the numbers they were saying? I asked. Tzedakah, he said. Donations, he said. A certain amount of money for the name of each of the dead, he said, and immediately I formed a commercial idea of the entire affair, understood that each name had its price. And how do you know how much each name costs? I asked my father, but he simply made a weary face and took a sip of coffee. I kept nibbling the cookie. Names of dead family members? I asked, and after a silence he said yes, but also dead friends, and dead soldiers, and the dead six million, and that number, for a Jew, even a Jew who's just a boy, needed no further explanation. Also the name of your brother Salomón, then, the one who drowned in the lake? I knew I was asking an illicit, even dangerous question. But I was thirteen now, I was all man now, I fasted now, I was now allowed to ask adults questions. My father observed me for a few seconds and I thought he was about to start crying. I don't know what you're talking about, he stammered, and left me alone with my cookie.

Sporadic drops continued to fall, as if the sky were still undecided about releasing the first rains of the year. The old dock swayed with each wave and each gust of wind, and it struck me that I was standing on the same wooden planks from which I'd dived so many times as a boy, and whispered that prayer so many times, and imagined so many times the floating lifeless body of the boy Salomón. The house looked identical to the house in my memory. The matilisguate tree on the shore was now huge and lush (I would have liked to remember the kind word I whispered on planting it). But the lake was no longer the deep blue lake of my childhood, nor was it the idyllic blue lake of my memory, but a thick pea soup.

Guayito, that's what I used to call you, right?

Don Isidoro was dressed in jeans—rolled halfway to his knee—a white cap with the Mayan Golf Club logo, and a gray t-shirt that was too big for him, with the faded green image of a tractor. He was holding a straw broom. His feet, on the old wooden planks, looked like two more planks.

And you and your brother used to call me Don Easypeasy-doro.

I'd completely forgotten that we called him that, and that he called me Guayito. But I smiled and shook his hand and said of course, Guayito, that's what you called me as a boy. Suddenly a fish jumped or spat on the greenish surface of the lake, as though mocking me and my lie. But Don Isidoro smiled in satisfaction. He had the smile of someone who tends toward melancholy. Then he let go of my hand and, after lowering his gaze, continued sweeping the dock's old planks. What can I do for you, young man?

WHAT I REMEMBER MOST about my father's factory in Florida, almost the only thing I remember, in fact, are all the naked women. Or rather, half-naked. Though for a boy it's the same thing. I remember the feeling of entering that old dirty warehouse and, as if it were the most normal thing, coming across women parading half-naked in high heels through the aisles and the waiting room and my father's office. I knew little about my father's factory. I knew that his partner was an old college friend, a Peruvian Jew, fat and unpleasant, who soon after ended up swindling him. I knew that the factory was located in a very Latino barrio called Hialeah—an hour from home, on the highway—and that they made women's bathing suits.

I knew that they constantly hired professional models to help promote their new products (my brother and I liked to sneak looks at the women in the catalogues that my father kept in a desk drawer as if they were forbidden magazines). I was still too young to look at those models with any sense of sexuality or even eroticism. But to a man, no matter his age, seminaked women are seminaked women and, as such, deserve our deepest concentration.

One Friday afternoon, after leaving school, I went with my mother to the factory in Hialeah to drop off some papers for my father. I was carrying them in a white folder. I had a party that night, one of my first parties with girls and music and sweaty hands, and I was anxious about being back in time to get ready. My mother was anxious, too, more anxious than usual. There was a lot of traffic on the highway, perhaps because it was Friday. I don't remember what comment I made to my mother in English—that she was going too slow or that it was already getting late or something like that—and she suddenly exploded. She began shouting at me in Spanish, loud, as though I'd insulted her. I shouldn't have said anything, but my comment really hadn't been that bad. I still wasn't old or mature enough, of course, to understand that her shouting had little to do with me: her father, my Polish grandfather, was in a hospital in Guatemala, beaten and injured after defending himself from two thieves who had tried to steal his black-stone ring (a symbol of mourning for his parents and siblings murdered in concentration camps) while he was walking down Avenida de las Américas; her mother, my grandmother, was recovering from surgery after a motorcycle had crashed into the door of her car, breaking her hip; and my father's factory in Hialeah, with all those naked and seminaked women, was on the brink of bankruptcy. My mother kept shouting at me. I actually thought she was on the verge of a nervous breakdown. And she was still shouting at me hysterically when, in the distance, we heard the blare of a siren. My mother pulled the Chevrolet station wagon over to the side of the highway.

The police officer, standing beside the car, told my mother that he'd clocked her driving too fast. My mother's face looked aflame. That can't be, she spat at the officer, her tone sassy, a bit rude. You were doing eighty, ma'am, in a sixty-mile zone. Impossible, that can't be, my mother reiterated, and I thought it better to close my eyes and simply listen as the officer asked for her license and car registration. You're wrong, my mother said to him (not shouting, but almost), and I closed my eyes tighter. For some reason, my mother always behaved that way with authority figures, with police and soldiers and civil servants and airport immigration officers, especially the Cuban ones in the Miami airport. Please step out of the car, ma'am. My mother didn't move. I'm not getting out of the car, she said

firmly. There was a long silence. All you could hear was
the buzz of traffic on the highway. Your documents,
ma'am. I opened my eyes and begged my mother
in Spanish to please give them to him. Ma'am, your
documents, the officer repeated, his voice softer and
more conciliatory. My mother called the police officer
insolent and, sighing and snorting loudly enough for
everyone on the highway to hear, she finally handed
her documents through the window. And I, just to do
something, just to distract myself, just because I'm a
coward, opened the white folder.

It was a long letter, on two typed pages. Both
pages, I still recall, had a huge weeping willow logo in
the upper right-hand corner, and the name of a cemetery or funeral home that I no longer recall or perhaps never knew. I began to read the letter, somewhat
bored by its somber and grandiose tone, until suddenly I came to the line where I saw Salomón's name.
And I closed the white folder.

The officer handed everything back to my mother
and told her that this time he would let her go with a
warning, but to please drive slower. My mother closed
the window without saying anything, and I smiled.
As usual, she'd gotten her way, triumphed in the face
of authority. My mother, I always knew, could disarm
any man with her beauty.

Back on the highway once more, I dared to ask
about the letter in the folder. It's nothing, she said

sharply, still angry with me or the police officer or the traffic or the whole of life. It was obvious that she wanted to smoke. She pulled off the highway, and suddenly everything turned more Latino, more boisterous. We were in Hialeah now. So why a letter from a funeral home? I asked in Spanish after a few minutes, in my most affectionate tone. It's about your father's brother, mi amor, she said finally. Salomón, I said quickly, and she turned to me and half-smiled, perhaps surprised I remembered that name, so seldom spoken. That's right, she said, Salomón. The one who died in the lake, I said quickly. My mother was no longer smiling. In the lake? she asked in confusion. What lake, mi amor? Amatitlán, I said. The boy Salomón, I said. The one who drowned in Lake Amatitlán. My mother parked in front of my father's factory and turned off the car engine. But he didn't die in a lake, she said. He died in New York, when he was a boy. And he's buried there, in New York, she said, pointing with her eyes to the papers in my hands.

New York? What do you mean, he died in New York? What do you mean, he's buried in New York? What about the boy floating in the lake, that pale naked boy whose face is tinged blue? What about the secret prayer on the dock?

But I didn't say anything. I didn't know what to say. I didn't even know what to think. The boy Salomón had died in the lake. Of that I was sure. Or at least I was sure that that's what I'd been told as a boy, in Guatemala. Or hadn't I?

The warehouse door opened and a group of half-naked women flew out toward us.

Where did you get that he died in the lake, mi amor?

Don Isidoro's granddaughter was standing at the large comal, placing tortillas down on its hot surface. From time to time, she'd pick up a small branch or a piece of ocote from the floor and toss it into the fire. Her name was Blanca. She was pregnant. She must have been about fifteen years old. She was the one who had opened the front gate. On the comal, a rusty pewter kettle was heating slowly.

Don Isidoro had invited me to have coffee at his house, which was more of a small improvised shack, made of cinder block and metal sheeting and a few loose boards. It was at the entrance to the property, just beside the black gate, like some kind of sentry box or security cabin. Don Isidoro and I were sitting on two wooden benches, on opposite sides of a rustic square table, on which there were a handful of dried beans and a few lotería game cards. The walls around us were made of adobe. The floor was rough cement slab. A small portable radio, hardly tuned to a marimba station, hung from a nail on the wall, halfway between one poster of the Virgin and another of Jesus.

Before us, Blanca moved in silence, as though floating from the comal to the single gas burner, and from the comal to two wicker baskets of fruit and vegetables, and from the comal to the cement sink painted red and full of dirty dishes. Eucalyptus leaves were smoking in a ceramic censer. Lying in one corner, the dog stared distrustfully or perhaps in anticipation at a hen on the other side of the open door, while it pecked at things on the ground in the yard, a thin cord tied to one of her feet. Each drop of rain reverberated on the corrugated metal roof, as if each drop of rain, as it fell, was yelling out its own name.

I don't know anything about that, Don Isidoro said to me when I finished recounting my memory—possibly false—of a boy drowned right there, by the dock. Young man, I didn't even know that your grandparents had had another boy, he whispered, combing his white hair with one hand. I said that yes, they had, that he would have been my father's older brother, that his name was Salomón. Imagine, he said, his voice adrift, so the boy was named Salomón, and Don Isidoro left his mouth open, and it struck me that he always looked as though he was about to forget the word he wanted to say. Suddenly, Blanca approached. She set two pewter cups and a plastic ashtray on the table, and Don Isidoro, as though his pregnant granddaughter was inciting him to smoke, took from the pocket of his pants a wrinkled pack of mentholated Rubios. I don't like mentholated cigarettes, but I accepted one just the same. Tell me, young man, you and your siblings grew up outside the country, right? Don Isidoro asked while exhaling smoke, and I said yes, we had, that we'd left the country as children, gone to the United States, and spent many years there. So many years, I told him, that at times I feel I'm no longer from here. Don Isidoro clicked his tongue a couple of times, smiling, wagging his head as though to indicate the totality of that which surrounded us. Young man, he said, you will always be from here. And we both smoked for a time in the quiet cacophony of the marimbas and the rain on the roof and the firewood crackling and the pewter kettle gurgling on the comal. Don Isidoro asked me what had happened to Salomón, and I told him that apparently he'd died in the United States, in New York, and that that's where he was buried. But what I don't quite understand, I told him, was why I grew up convinced that he had drowned here in Amatitlán, as a boy, near the dock. I don't know if I imagined it or I dreamed it all, I told him, and even my voice sounded strange to me. I don't know if that's what someone told me, I said to him, to deceive me, or to tease me, or to frighten me, or perhaps to keep me away from the edge of the lake. I fell silent and smoked long and deep, as if the mentholated smoke was oxygen, while in my mind I shuffled once more through each of the hypotheses that justified or explained my memory—possibly false—of a boy drowned close to the dock, and repeating to myself that, according to epicurean epistemology, if there exist several possible explanations to explain a phenomenon, you must retain them all.

Don Isidoro's cigarette hung from his lower lip. He was arranging the lotería game cards on the table and giving me the look of a boy who doesn't know the answer, or who knows the answer very well but doesn't dare say it.

Blanca poured coffee into the two pewter cups. She put the kettle back on the comal and stayed there, at the comal, encouraging the flames with a fan made of palm frond. The coffee tasted of mist.

I do remember a boy who drowned in the lake in those years, Don Isidoro said suddenly as he smoked. Not here, but on the other side of the bay, over by the village of Tacatón. He raised his pewter cup and downed half of the coffee in a single swallow. They said the boy fell off a boat, he said, in the middle of the lake, and that no one on the boat realized. Don Isidoro took another long swallow, set the empty cup on the table. His little body finally turned up a few days later, on the shore in Tacatón, he said. The lake took care to push him out, he said. Or at least that's what the villagers claimed. But I wouldn't know, he said as a kind of full stop, and mashed his cigarette out in the plastic ashtray. I asked him if Tacatón was far, and he said not very. I asked him if he remembered what year the boat accident had happened, and he simply scratched the back of his neck and shook his head. I asked him if it had been a local boy or a boy from the capital, and he said from the capital, then he said local, then he said he didn't remember too well. I asked him if he knew the boy's name, and Don Isidoro coughed a couple of times: a hoarse cough, rasping, with echoes of sadness. That I couldn't say, young man.

Blanca tossed a fresh eucalyptus branch onto the coal in the censer, then walked toward us in silence, carrying the kettle.

What if that boy was also named Salomón? she asked while refilling my cup. I didn't say anything, unsure whether I was more surprised at her voice, so sweet and docile, or at her words, the first since we'd sat down. Maybe, Blanca continued as she now filled her grandfather's cup, you just confused two dead little boys because both of them were named Salomón.

Don Isidoro reached out a hand, placed it gently on his granddaughter's round belly, and left it there.

SOME TIME BEFORE TRAVELING by car to Amatitlán, I called my brother at his house in the south of France to tell him that I wanted to go to the lake (or perhaps I told him that I needed to go) to look for our grandparents' house. My brother first said something that I didn't manage to hear properly due to the poor international connection, then asked me where I was. I told him New York, just passing through. I thought about telling him that I was passing through in order to rendezvous with a secret lover, to attend an afternoon of jazz at an apartment in Harlem, to search for clues to a forbidden grave, to receive Guggenheim money that I'd then spend on a trip to Germany and Poland, to Łódź. But all I asked him was if he still remembered the lake house in Amatitlán. Not really, he said. I asked him if he still remembered the words to the secret prayer that we'd invented as kids and that we whispered on the dock before diving in to swim in the water. What secret prayer? my brother asked. The secret prayer we invented in Amatitlán, I said, somewhat confused, to scare off the ghost of the boy Salomón. What boy Salomón? my brother asked. I was on the verge of reciting, shouting, the entire prayer to him. Then I was on the verge of asking if he was smoking something. But luckily I contained myself in time and asked only if he truly didn't remember the boy Salomón, our grandparents' firstborn son, the one who would have been our father's older brother. My brother remained quiet for a few seconds. As though processing my words. Or as though my words were taking a few seconds to find their way from New York to the south of France. Or as though he was concentrating on rolling a good joint. Our father had an older brother?

I don't know if I was more captivated by his sky blue eyes or by the idea that he'd been in jail.

His name was Emile. He was my Lebanese grandfather's younger brother. He lived with his new wife in a crumbling building on Alton Road, in Miami Beach, not too far from our house, and just a few blocks from the shop of Aunt Lynda, their younger sister. Taking advantage of the fact that my grandparents were spending a few days with us—I don't remember whether on vacation or to help my father out with the problems at the factory—Uncle Emile had invited us all to dinner at an Italian restaurant in his neighborhood, right on the beach (Aunt Lynda, as usual, had begged off). The restaurant's owner, a fat guy named Sal, was his friend or partner—it wasn't too clear to me which. Big Sal, they called him. Years later, when Big Sal turned up dead on the beach with a rose on his chest, I finally understood that he was part of Miami's Italian Mafia.

That night was the first time I met Uncle Emile. It may have been the first time I realized he existed. And the moment I got there and saw him standing at the restaurant's turquoise-colored entrance, so elegant as he smoked a cigar beside his friend or partner, it became clear why no one had ever mentioned him.

So you're little Eduardo, he said to me in English, still outside the restaurant. He was dressed in a silver-gray suit, white shirt, black tie and equally black handkerchief folded into the pocket of his jacket. His cuff links, impossible to forget, were two big emeralds set in gold. He had thin, completely white hair, the bluest eyes I had ever seen, and one of those long, straight noses whose tip seems always to be pointing the way. I didn't understand how my Lebanese grandfather could have a brother so distinguished, so handsome. This is for you, Uncle Emile said, handing me a package. Happy birthday, he said, and the gesture surprised me. I had turned fourteen a couple of months earlier, but I still accepted and thanked him for the gift. We'll head inside, Uncle Emile announced to the group, one arm over my shoulders, and he didn't let me go the rest of the night.

It was evident, even to me, that my grandfather and his brother didn't get along. They began to argue when we sat down (several times they mentioned Aunt Lynda's name, in a whisper, as if it were a forbidden name), their voices already somewhat sharp, their recriminations sometimes in French, sometimes in English, sometimes in Arabic. Edouard, that's what Uncle Emile called my grandfather, in French, the language they'd learned in Beirut, as kids, during the French occupation. Behind us, on a small platform, a woman with enormous breasts and too much makeup was singing opera arias, a cappella, in Italian. I was sitting beside Uncle Emile, who every once in a while would break off his conversation with the adults to ask me a question or tell me to look at the singer's legs or give me a bite of one of his favorite antipasti or a secret sip of his grappa. And I was trying it all enthusiastically as the recriminations between him and my grandfather grew louder, and as I watched the way Uncle Emile's pale, delicate fingers—always to the beat of the music—seemed to play the keys of an imaginary piano on the white tablecloth.

After a while the waiter arrived with a chocolate cake. The woman got down off the platform and sang to me in Italian from very close, stroking my hair with a chubby hand, and it all felt a bit absurd two months after my birthday. Then the same waiter returned and left a small cup of espresso before Uncle Emile, who immediately, as he lit a cigar, leaned toward me, reached his arm around my shoulders, and pulled me close. He wanted to tell me something without the others hearing.

Go on, open your present, he whispered with a slight smile. But do it in secret, he added, playing a brief melody on the white tablecloth. And I happily obeyed. I placed the package in my lap and ripped the paper off very slowly, without making any noise, and without anyone seeing me. It was a book. I think Uncle Emile saw the disappointment on my face, because he let out a quick little laugh. Look inside, he whispered, index finger to his lips.

IT WAS LIKE SEEING my grandfather dressed as a woman.

Her name was Lynda, her shop a small place selling tablecloths and lace on Lincoln Road, in Miami Beach, Lynda's House of Linen. She was the youngest sibling, and almost identical to my grandfather. They had the same wide, stocky body, the same hands, the same skin, so pale that it looked pink, the same Lebanese accent (their words fell to the world like slabs of steel), exactly the same walk. My father liked to take my brother and me to visit her at her shop in Miami Beach some Saturday afternoons, and we let ourselves be taken grudgingly, moodily, forced to sacrifice our Saturday for a couple of hours of boredom in that shop, hot and stuffy and smelling of old people. But right next door, luckily, was a glimmering bubble-gum pink ice cream parlor.

That afternoon, as soon as she saw us come in, Aunt Lynda had run to greet my brother and me at the door, to hug us, to cover our faces in red lipstick. Then she'd taken us by the hand and led us behind the counter and, as she did every time we went to visit her, she'd given us a fine white cotton handkerchief, probably a sample or remnant. We never knew what to do with that handkerchief (secretly we joked that it was to wipe the red lipstick from our faces), a handkerchief that we were furthermore supposed to share. But we thanked her just the same and sat on two high stools to watch Aunt Lynda sell tablecloths to the froufrou women of

Miami Beach (years later we would realize that her business was a gold mine, and that Aunt Lynda was a great businesswoman), waiting anxiously for my father to tell us that we could go for an ice cream next door.

It wasn't my fault.

Aunt Lynda's English always sounded like machete blows to me, almost angry, and these last words even more so. It wasn't my fault, do you understand? she repeated to my father. She was standing behind the counter, working the cash register. Her face was red, her expression nervous, her white hair a bit unkempt. But I never said it was your fault, my father whispered to her, his voice quiet and soothing, perhaps in order to calm her, or perhaps so that my brother and I wouldn't hear what they were talking about. All of you have always thought it was my fault, Aunt Lynda shouted, her hand in the air, as though swearing loyalty, or as though signaling with her hand at all those who'd thought her guilty. But guilty of what? What was she talking about? All of you, she yelled at my father, but especially your mother, and the cash register rang, echoing her. My brother was saying something to me from his stool. I was trying to ignore him in order to pay attention, until he hit me on the leg and stammered to look quick, there, in front of us. A young blond woman was leaning over a table full of tablecloths, her blouse loose and partially open, and from our angle we could clearly see one of her breasts. Salomón was not my responsibility, you understand? said Aunt Lynda, now quieter, more conciliatory. The young woman bent over a bit farther (she looked like a model or an actress), and her blouse opened a bit more (she might not have been wearing a bra), and I couldn't stop looking at the pale glimmer of her breast (I felt, as always, the tingle of lust around my mouth), while I heard Aunt Lynda say something about New Jersey, about Atlantic City, about being a newlywed back then, about living far from the boy Salomón when the boy Salomón died in New York. I kept trying to order her words, to make some kind of sense of them, while I watched the woman as she straightened up, smoothed her long blond hair with her hand, arranged her blouse and, after shooting a furtive glance in our direction, slowly exited the shop. What happened in New York was not my fault, Aunt Lynda insisted, and my father, downcast, his arms crossed, simply remained silent. And I understood that silence of my father's not as insecurity, or as hesitation, or even as defeat, but as a way to protect my brother and me from something much larger than us, from something sinister that was approaching.

I DON'T REMEMBER what book Uncle Emile gave me that night in that Italian restaurant in Miami Beach, and I'm sure that he, if he were alive, wouldn't remember, either. The book, I suspect, was simply his excuse to give me the thing that was inside, and that I've held on to and taken care of since then. Uncle Emile, with the pride of a musketeer, had slipped into the book a newspaper clipping that recounted the deed that had sent him to prison.

Today I'd like to believe that he gave it to me as a special gift, unique, for me alone. But I doubt it. Instead, I picture him that same afternoon sitting in his apartment on Alton Road, opening his desk drawer and taking out one of the hundreds of newspaper clippings that recounted his story and that he kept stored there, in order to parcel them out as gifts all across the world. That night, then, enthralled and ignoring all the screaming in the background from the opera singer and my grandfather and my grandmother and Uncle Emile, I read the story—for the first of many times—of how Uncle Emile, in 1960, passing himself off as a Las Vegas gambler named John McGurney, had swindled a Miami millionairess.

The story said that first Uncle Emile had seduced the woman, Genevra McAllister, a widow ten years his senior, and then another of the incriminated men, a guy from Chicago named Albert George, had dressed up as a Catholic priest and married them. Father Leon, the guy called himself, the story said. Then Albert George and Uncle Emile, with the help of two Miami brothers by the last name of Adjmis, convinced the woman to buy a lingerie factory in France. A factory where the lingerie was made by nuns, the story said, and benefited orphaned children. A nonexistent factory, the story said. Then the four men convinced the woman to start buying up the whole town in France, insisting that that way she'd help to keep the town from being taken over by a German named Finkelstein. The story said that the McAllister woman believed that she was not only helping nuns and orphaned children but saving the entire town from Finkelstein the German. A town and a German both nonexistent, the story said. The McAllister woman stated at the trial that it was as if she had been in a fog, that the four men had arrived and brought lights and cocktail parties back into her widow's life. And then, little by little, she began handing over all her money: over $1.2 million, it was estimated. The four men, the story said, were sentenced to five years in prison.

When I finished reading and looked up, my grandmother was no longer at the table (later they explained to me that she'd gone off to the rest room, furious). My grandfather was now standing, shouting something at Uncle Emile, who was still sitting beside me and shouting back at my grandfather. My father was attempting to calm them. Big Sal was attempting to calm them. My mother had one hand over her mouth and was about to start crying. My brother, far from me, on the other side of the table, looked scared. The woman on the platform kept singing her sad aria.

And it occurred to me, listening to all of them shout, that two brothers could not be more different. My grandfather was honorable, hardworking, so loyal to his family that he always ended up helping them and saving them (many years afterward I'd learn that my grandfather not only sent his brother a monthly stipend but that later, after Uncle Emile died, he kept sending the same amount every month to his widow), whereas Uncle Emile sailed through life without a single responsibility, from woman to woman, from party to party, maybe from swindle to swindle. I don't remember why they were fighting that night; maybe I never knew, since it was impossible for me to understand the shouting in Arabic and French. All I remember is that suddenly my grandfather shouted something in Arabic and Uncle Emile shook his head and stood up, stubbing out his cigar in a silver ashtray. For the first time that night, the woman stopped singing. And I realized then that dinner was over. The two brothers were staring right at each other, in silence, like two gunslingers each challenging the other to fire. Everything froze for a few seconds. Everybody in the restaurant fell silent for a few seconds, long enough for the last thing shouted in English by Uncle Emile to resonate throughout the entire restaurant, while he pointed at my grandfather with much more than his index finger. And you, Edouard, he shouted, you abandoned your son Salomón.

THE NARROW STREETS OF TACATÓN were empty. The only pedestrians I found, and whom I tried to ask a question from the car, simply moved off distrustfully. I decided to park the Saab right on the road, in front of a little plaza painted yellow and green, with two soccer goals, two basketball hoops, a yellow church at one end and at the other a round fountain that had no water, as though there for adornment. I remained seated in the car for a few minutes, watching the raindrops disappear the moment they hit something—the church's yellow wall or the ground in the plaza or the car windshield— and I realized that all of those raindrops, more than disappearing, were actually exploding. I remained still, concentrating on the glass, listening to all those white explosions. An endless string of white explosions in the now-dark Tacatón afternoon. But explosions not like bombs, or like gunshots, and not like fireworks, either, more like an infinite series of cymbals in a great white symphony.

After a while I got out of the car and walked a few blocks in the rain. On one side of the road was a row of small, corrugated sheet-metal shacks that looked like they didn't belong there, like they'd spontaneously cropped up. A barber's shop, a tire repair, a carpenter's workshop (we make antiques, the sign said), a pan dulce and champurrada stand, a stall painted navy blue, with writing on the front—big black letters—that said they upholstered motorcycle seats, repaired shoes, sold coconuts at five quetzals each, blew boulders up with dynamite. But there were no people. All the shacks were closed. I quickly crossed the cobbled street toward the only open door, the one place I saw that wasn't closed at that time of the afternoon. And the moment I walked through the door, I regretted it.

A fat mustachioed man was shooting pool. In the corner, watching him play from a plastic chair, sat a very young woman, maybe a girl or a teenager, dressed in a red miniskirt and white high heels. One long black braid hung over each shoulder. She was holding something dark on her lap. It looked to me, maybe because of the way she was splayed in the chair, like she was crying or had been crying. Beside her, two more women were dancing slowly, holding each other tight. An old man was leaning against the back wall, in the darkest part of the place, simply watching the two women dance, and I thought I saw in the darkness that the old man's face was made-up. But made-up completely white, like a clown's. It struck me that perhaps the place was a cantina. Or a pool hall. Or a brothel. I wasn't sure. I could hardly see. The only light was what was coming in through the open door behind me. A ranchera played on a radio in the distance.

Did the general send you? the fat man asked without looking at me, bending over the table, about to take a shot. His question confused me, and I was about to say something when I managed to distinguish a black object on the green felt of the table, which I first took to be the little radio playing the ranchera, but then, when my eyes adapted to the dim light, I saw or thought I saw that it was a gun. I said did the general send you? the man asked again, a bit louder, straightening up now and giving me a hard stare. The two women had stopped dancing and also watched me. The made-up old man shouted something from the back of the place, perhaps a threat or an insult, and then began to approach the pool table. He was coming straight toward me. But the man with the mustache signaled to him with his hand (as though saying this asshole is all mine) and the made-up old man stumbled back to the far wall. I couldn't or didn't want to move my eyes from what was possibly a gun on the green felt, in the middle of the table, in the middle of a game, as if it were one more ball, but soon I managed to regain my composure and stammered to the man that no, that I was sorry, that I was just looking for someplace to eat. It was the first thing that came into my mind, as an excuse. The two women embraced once more. The man, after a sigh, returned to his game of pool. Up the road, on the right, he said brusquely, I'm not sure whether disappointed or annoyed. I thanked him. And as I was already stepping back toward the open door, already feeling the raindrops once again, the dark thing on the girl's lap jumped down to the floor and meowed at me.

It was a small place with no name, or at least no visible name. The walls, painted the same green as the plaza, were full of posters and pennants for Gallo beer (almost all featuring women in bikinis). There were no tables or chairs, just a long crude pine counter with four high stools. An old man was sitting at one of the stools: languid, hunched over, his face almost in the soup that sat steaming before him. On another stool, a teenager had his head down on the counter, asleep or perhaps drunk. A short chubby woman was watching television behind the counter. Immediately she turned it off and stood.

Good afternoon, she said to me with a half smile full of sorrow and gold. I greeted her, drying my face on my shirtsleeve and taking a seat on another of the stools, and ordered a beer. The old man didn't even look up. Is Gallo alright? she asked, and I said yes, thank you. The woman opened the glass door of a small refrigerator and took out a bottle. Can I get you something to eat? she said as she wiped and dried the bottle with her apron and then set it on the counter in front of me. I asked her what the soup was that the man was eating. It's a stew, she said. Chirín, it's called. Our typical dish here. I saw that the broth in the enormous bowl was full of hunks of fish, carrots, half ears of corn, whole crab. Very tasty, the old man whispered without looking at me, his hands gripping the thin claws of a crab. And listening to the old man suck the claws, I imagined that all of that fish and sea-food was from right there, and that the old man was sucking toxic lake water. There's also creole chicken and rice, said the woman. There's chiles rellenos, fried bream, tamales, some nice black beans. The drunk guy grunted something, then went back to sleep. I noticed that on the pine counter sat a red plastic dish of what looked like roasted peanuts, but rounder and darker, almost like burned coffee beans, and I asked the woman what they were. Zompopos de mayo, she said. Leaf-cutter ants. Nice and toasted, she said, with salt and lime. I took a sip of beer and said that I'd never tried them before, that I'd never seen them cooked, that I didn't even know how they were made. The woman explained that first you had to put them all on the comal, to kill them with the heat of the comal, before you started taking off their wings and legs and heads. One by one, she said. Lots of work, she said. See, you only eat the round body of each zompopo, she said, holding an invisible little ball up between her thumb and index finger. Anyway, then you put the zompopo bodies back on the comal and toast them nice and slow, with salt and lime. Go on, try them, she said, pushing the dish toward me. And then I, reaching out a hand and trying one zompopo abdomen and then another (salty, crunchy, with a hint of pork-crackling flavor), could only think of the zompopo fights that

my brother and I had organized as kids. Each May,
after the first rains, the garden filled with the huge
angry leaf-cutters, and we, in the afternoons, after getting back from school, would stick two of them in
a little cardboard box or in a lunch box—their own
miniature ring—and they would immediately turn to
each other and begin to fight. Sometimes to the death.
Sometimes we'd place bets. You don't see so many of
them anymore, the old man mumbled, the claws still
in his hands. They're hard to find, said the woman, you
don't see so many here in town or in the mountains or
around the lake. I was going to tell them that maybe
you didn't see as many zompopos as before because of
the shrinking forests in the mountains, or because of
the overuse of chemicals and pesticides, or because of
all the boys who used to make them fight to the death
in our lunch boxes. But I simply took a long sip of
beer. All three of us remained silent for a moment,
and I took advantage of that silence to ask them if by
chance they recalled a boy who had drowned there,
or near there, in the seventies. Oh no, the woman said
quickly, almost without even listening to the question,
as if the very question of a dead boy had frightened
her. The old man simply kept sucking and slurping
the claws. After taking another sip of beer, I told them
that I was looking for someone who might remember that boy, whose body, according to what I'd been
told, turned up floating on the shore in Tacatón. The

woman shot a furtive glance at the old man, a glance that lasted no longer than a fraction of a second but that was full of suspicion or distrust. And it struck me, in that fraction of a second, that they may have judged me a policeman, or an army officer, or a government representative, and that even if they knew anything, they wouldn't tell me. Then I took a sip of lukewarm beer and, in my best baritone, told them: The boy who drowned in the lake was my father's brother.

The old man stopped sucking toxic water. The woman, her expression now pious, crossed herself. And I convinced myself that I was not deceiving them, that it was not a lie, that it was a version of the story that had at one point been true, at least to me.

Maybe Doña Ermelinda remembers something, said the old man. Yes, maybe, the woman added. That old witch remembers everything, the old man said, giving a little laugh somewhere between timid and rueful. I asked them where I could find her, if she lived in town. She lives right here, Doña Erme does, said the woman. Her house is a little ways down, by the lake. But who knows if she's there, she added. She goes out to the mountain a lot to search for her leaves. The drunk guy grunted once more. He was drooling on the counter. Give me a minute and I'll show you the way, said the old man without looking at me, the clay bowl in his hands as he sipped a watery yellow broth. I told him that was very kind of him. I took out a couple of bills and gave them to the woman and told her that I'd pay for the man's stew, and he muttered something between sips. Then he set the bowl on the counter, wiped his graying mustache with one hand, placed his straw hat on his head, and very quietly, I don't know whether sincere or mocking, added: May God protect you.

ON A COVERED PATIO, atop a table or altar, between a hemp-rope hammock and a couple of plastic chairs, stood a doll in a black suit and black hat, surrounded by candles of all colors and unlit votive lamps and white eggs and hand-rolled cigars and an eighth of Quezalteca firewater and the decapitated and still bloody head of a turkey.

We'd walked there along a path so narrow only one person could fit. I was behind the old man, following his straw hat in the rain, when he told me that Doña Ermelinda was a sobadora. I told him I'd never heard that word, and the old man explained to me that she was a healer, but that people in town called her a soba-dora because to cure their sicknesses she rubbed their skin with oils and tinctures and ointments she made herself. Any ailment, the old man said. Burns, cuts, fevers, pregnancies, cancers, he said. Mainly she uses herbs and roots, he said. But sometimes she uses other things, he said, and I chose not to ask anything more.

I'd been waiting for her for an hour, beneath the

branches of an araucaria tree, smoking. The rain was now a silk curtain, barely perceptible but constant. There was a motionless cayuco, a small wooden canoe, in the water, far off, its black outline barely visible in the shadow of dusk. A village began to twinkle on the other side of the lake. Behind me, the whole mountain was the shriek of a single bat. I kept watching the water, so dark and serene at that hour of the evening, and soon it struck me that right there, at the bottom of the lake, lay my black plastic watch, still timing, still waiting to reach the end point of that straight line, that final surfboard ride. And I was still smoking, trying not to get too wet or to pay much attention to the fresh blood on the covered patio floor, when finally I saw the old woman appear on the shoreline. I mashed my cigarette out on the ground.

She was walking slowly, swaying from side to side, hobbling, as if one of her legs was a bit longer than the other. She was barefoot. Her straight silver hair flowed from a headpiece, a pearl blue tocoyal, and reached all the way to her hips. She was dressed in traditional clothing, a wraparound skirt and beautiful white huipil embroidered with green and blue flowers, a black shawl over her shoulders. On her back she carried a large pack, heavy, perhaps full of roots and herbs. And as I watched her approach slowly along the lakeshore, I got the impression that the old woman was growing thinner, and thinner still, until before my eyes the whole

of her had become a small skeleton. Her leather skin
had disappeared completely and I could clearly see the
bones that were Doña Ermelinda. Her jawbone. Her
cheekbones. Her hips and ribs. Each minuscule bone
of her little owl feet.

The old lady let the pack drop onto the wet earth
and, breathing loudly, almost panting, spat at me: You're
here looking for a drowned boy. Her words wrapped
my head in cellophane. I quickly pulled the cellophane
off and got my breath back and was about to blather
that indeed I was, that that was me, that no doubt the
woman from the cafeteria had said something to her
already, or that the old man in the straw hat had spoken
of me, but the old woman's tremulous voice beat me to
it. Last night I dreamed that you were right here, she
said, under my araucaria tree.

HE HAS NO ARMS because the campesinos hacked them
off with machetes.

Doña Ermelinda was still kneeling before the altar,
lighting the many-colored candles and votive lamps
around Maximón. She told me that Maximón had
been a very handsome saint who performed miracles
and easily seduced all the women. But when the wom-
en's husbands found out, she told me, they hacked off
his arms, just macheted them right off. That's why he
has no arms, she said, showing me the empty sleeves of

the doll's black suit. But he still dances, she said. Still smokes. Likes to drink. Has lots of money. And Max- imón owns everything, the old woman said, and con- tinued lighting the candles around the effigy. I asked her if the candles' colors had any significance, and Doña Ermelinda, without looking at me, told me that the blue ones were the heart of the sky, and the green ones were the heart of the earth, and the red ones were the skin, and the yellow ones were corn, when they were good, and sickness, when they were bad. And the black candles? I asked her, and Doña Ermelinda told me that one must not speak of the black ones. Looking at her in silence in the semidarkness, it struck me that each one of her movements was slow and deliberate, as though it hurt, or as though she was moving against the wind, or as though her skeleton hands were no longer in any hurry to get anywhere. Still kneeling, she took one of the cigars, lit it with a candle's flame and blew smoke twice over the effigy. Then, after filling her mouth with Quezalteca, she spat up a cloud of firewater. She put the bottle back in its place while whispering words to the doll in a Mayan language, perhaps Kaqchikel or Poqomchí (words that sounded to me neither solemn nor ceremonious, but cautionary). Finally she stood with difficulty and went to sit in the other plastic chair. Her bare feet didn't reach the floor.

SHE TOLD ME THAT the drowned boy was not named Salomón, but Juan Pablo Herrera Irigoyen, and that he'd fallen from the boat without anyone noticing. Latest-model boat, she told me, high speed. The family was out for a boat ride around the lake. The boy was three years old. He was the son of a wealthy farmer from the capital whose coffee plantation spanned— spans—one whole side of the volcano. We found his little body here on the shore, the old woman told me, the following day, as soon as the sun came out. The boy was naked. He had no life vest. Some time later the father came to town in the same boat and had a white marble cross built in the exact spot where his son's body had been found. I can show you later, if you like.

SHE TOLD ME THAT another drowned boy was also not named Salomón, but Luis Pedro Rodríguez Batz. He was from Villa Canales. He'd drowned while he and some friends were jumping into the lake from the rock at the now-abandoned Dorión castle. That's what people here call the medieval-style castle built by Don Carlos Dorión Nanne in 1935, the old woman told me, on a magnificent cliff given to him by the dictator at that time, Jorge Ubico, who then used the castle's cellar, they say, to torture his enemies and prisoners. The boy Luis Pedro was ten years old. The other boys, up at the castle, thought that the body floating below in the lake was a practical joke.

SHE TOLD ME THAT another drowned boy was also not named Salomón, but Juan Romero Martínez Estrada. His father, a young evangelical pastor in the small village of Mesillas Altas, was known around the lake for his Sunday sermons, in which he spoke fervently of the poor, of social injustice, of the lack of equality. He and his wife disappeared one night, the old woman told me, and no one ever heard anything about them again. Some people in Mesillas Altas say that they saw them after midnight on the road that runs from the village to San Vicente Pacaya, accompanied by a troop of soldiers, and they think the young couple were disappeared in the volcano crater. Days later the body of their only son was found at the shore of the lake. They say the boy Juan Romero looked like he was sleeping on the ground. He was still in his pajamas. He hadn't yet turned one.

SHE TOLD ME THAT another drowned boy was also not named Salomón, but Francisco Alfonso Caballero Ochoa. He was eleven years old. They called him Paquito. He was rowing a wooden cayuco with his little brother, on the western side of the lake, when he lost one of his oars in the water. His brother says that he saw him dive in after the oar, and that was the last time he saw him. His body never surfaced, the old woman told me. But there are those who say they still see the boy Paquito, she told me, or the spirit of the boy Paquito. He's always walking half-naked along the shore of the lake, they say. Still looking for his oar.

She told me that another drowned boy was also not named Salomón, but Marco Tulio Ruata Gaytán. He was six years old. He'd been playing with a soccer ball, she told me, all alone, on an empty field near the Plátanos River. The last person to see him alive was his mother. His mother said that the boy Marco Tulio was kicking his ball against the wall of the school and she shouted at him to stop, to go play with the ball some-place else instead. No one heard anything about him for two days, until his body turned up there by the landfill crossing, where the train line comes through, the old woman told me. He was lying on a bed of water lilies, his little legs tangled up in some fisher-man's sky blue trammel netting.

She told me that another drowned boy was also not named Salomón and was also not a boy, but a girl named María José Pérez Huité. She was eleven years old.

They called her Joselita. Along with her father and a few other men from Santa Elena Barillas, she formed part of a mariachi band known as El Mariachi Pérez. The girl Joselita played guitar and sang. She was the only girl in the band. She always wore a beautiful maroon suit covered in gold sequins, while the men wore the typical black mariachi costume. It's thought that the girl Joselita fell into the lake one night during a storm, near where the Michatoya River flows out, after the band finished a serenade. Her father said that the girl had gotten lost in the night, by the lake, and that she didn't know how to swim. The following morning, someone from town was crossing the La Gloria bridge when they saw, down in the river, a spot of maroon floating.

SHE TOLD ME THAT another drowned boy was also not named Salomón, but Juan Cecilio López Mijangos. He drowned during the aquatic procession of the Baby Jesus of Amatitlán, though nobody knows how. He was seven years old. He was from the village of Chichimecas. He was with his parents and siblings, she told me, sitting in a rowboat as part of the procession, while all of the rowboats were taking Zarquito to his rock throne, over on the stone wall known as Los Órganos. That's what people here call the doll of the Baby Jesus used in the procession, Zarquito—Baby Blue—apparently because he has such light eyes, the old woman told me. One night, according to the legend, the Baby Jesus appeared to some fishermen in the middle of the lake, sitting in a chair and surrounded by light, and they decided to bring him back to Pampichín, their town on the southern bank of the lake. Beginning around that time, some mornings people started seeing little footprints of the Baby Jesus on the ground in front of the parish church, or over by the landfill crossing, or around the Baby Jesus' chair. And also since around that time, she told me, in order to honor him, they have had an aquatic pilgrimage across the lake every third of May. Some say that in that particular year, at the end of the procession, the boy Juan Cecilio fell from the boat without anyone in the crowd noticing, so concentrated were they all on praying to Zarquito. Others say that one of his brothers pushed him into the water, out of pure wickedness. Still others say they themselves saw how the boy Juan Cecilio dived into the water from the boat and insisted on swimming to the stone chair at Los Órganos, where Zarquito was already seated. Los Órganos, the old woman told me, is at the deepest part of the lake.

She told me that another boy who drowned during the aquatic procession of the Baby Jesus, the most recent one, the one last year, was also not named Salomón, but Juan Luis Recopalchí Blanco. The boy Juan Luis

was ten years old. He was sitting in one of the boats
that follow the aquatic procession, the old woman told
me, along with twenty-five other passengers, all going
back to Amatitlán after having left Zarquito there on
his rock at Los Órganos. Several people were standing
on the town's public dock, watching the boat get closer,
waiting for their family members, and they testified the
following. That first they'd heard how the boat's owner
and pilot advised the passengers to head to the front of
the vessel. That then they'd heard how some passengers
began to shout that the boat was leaking. That then
they'd seen how the whole boat tipped onto its left side.
And that within seconds the whole boat had already
disappeared completely into the water. None of the
passengers was wearing a life vest. But they were a few
meters from the public dock, and all of them managed
to swim those few meters and save themselves. All, the
old woman said, except the boy Juan Luis. His lifeless
body was found that afternoon by the team of frogmen
from the volunteer fire brigade. The authorities deter-
mined that the boat had sunk due to excess weight.
Diana, the boat was named. The owner and pilot, the
old woman told me, was the boy's father.

I ASKED HER WHAT HERBS OR ROOTS she'd put in, but
Doña Ermelinda simply told me that I should drink
slowly, that it would help me see the truth. Her face

shone crimson in the night. The three or four logs on the fire crackled and sparked. Behind me, from an angel's trumpet bush hung a good number of white bell-shaped flowers. I wanted to ask her what truth, or which one of all truths, or whose truth exactly. But I simply kept watching Doña Ermelinda in the amber light of the patio, feeling both incredulous and skeptical, and took a hot sip from the small gourd bowl. It tasted like burned water. I took a second sip, which tasted even more unpleasant than the first, and at the same time I was overcome by a strange sense of levity, of sleepiness, of being and not being. The old woman gazed at me firmly, her brow furrowed, as though attempting to understand or decipher something. It will help you see your truth, she said suddenly from her plastic chair, as though responding to the questions in my head. I got a bit scared. I felt slightly dizzy. I felt that my eyes were closing and a part of me began to float. Not the truth of the drowned boy, the old woman said. Your truth of yours, she said, with that double possessive so common among indigenous speakers. Perhaps the old woman noticed the fear or confusion on my face, because immediately she told me that the wisest of the Mayans, after creating all the things in the world, realized that there was no mud or corn left. So they searched for a jade stone and whittled it until they formed a little arrow, and when the wise ones blew on the arrow, it turned into a hummingbird, and the hummingbird took off and flew the entire world. Tz'unun, said the old woman. That's what we call it, in our language, she said, and fell silent for a moment. It's the hummingbird, she then said, who flies from here to there with the thoughts of man.

I broke my brother's foot.

We'd gone two or three years without speaking, in either English or in Spanish. Nothing monumental had taken place to drive us apart. No rupture, no single specific fight. We'd simply grown distant. Or rather, I had distanced myself from him. I was older—fourteen months older, which in adolescence is much more than fourteen months—and I remember that suddenly, at about thirteen, I started to find him too childish. Before, we'd done everything together. We'd been kids together and grown up together like two allies or two best friends. We'd shared a room, whispering from bed to bed so that the darkness of the night wasn't as dark, until I demanded my own room and my parents had to remodel the den. We'd played in the tub together, making each nighttime bath an adventure with pirates or sailors, until I opted to use my parents' shower, and left him alone in the tub. We'd worn the same clothes, until I demanded to dress differently from him. We'd kept our toys mixed together, our marble and stamp collections, until I insisted we separate everything and divvy it up (then I threw my half in the trash, rather than give it to him). I felt like an adult, too big to put up with his boyish company, his comments and childish games, and then I not only moved away from him but I began to insult him, to treat him as less, perhaps in order to push him even further away. I don't know when it happened, or why, but now everything between us was a battle.

My brother's broken foot was the culmination of an entire Sunday of insults, and rows, and bad moods, and a basketball game on the street with several of my neighborhood friends, during which I suddenly made fun of my brother. A stupid joke, meaningless, that would have blown over like any other joke—one more insult from an older brother who takes advantage of his age and his size—had it not been for the cutting laughter of my friends. My friends kept laughing. And as their laughter at my joke grew, I could clearly see the anger on my brother's face rising: in the veins on his neck, in his trembling lips, in his flushed cheeks, in his tensed-up expression, in all the little drops of sweat that began to form on his brow. And I knew that the kick was coming. I knew it before my brother raised his leg. I probably knew it before he himself knew that he should kick me hard in the stomach, to knock the breath and voice out of me and also to silence my friends' malicious laughter. His right foot, then, smashed against my elbow.

My mother took him to the hospital. My father, making an effort not to shout, simply told me to go to my room, said that we'd talk later, that for the time being he couldn't even look at me. I shut myself in and lay down on the bed with my headphones on and spent the rest of the afternoon listening to music. I didn't understand the gravity of the situation. I didn't find out that my brother had broken his foot until that night, when my father finally came to tell me. My mother had called from the hospital, I had broken my brother's foot, he informed me from the doorway. But he tried to kick me, I said to my father in English, still lying down. All I did was defend myself from his kick, I said. It wasn't my fault, I said, though I knew perfectly well that it had indeed been my fault, that who was at fault had nothing to do with my brother's kick, or with defending myself, or with his broken foot, but with something much more profound and Biblical, with something that only two brothers can understand. My father continued standing in the doorway. It doesn't matter whose fault it was, he said. In his voice there was more sadness than fury, more disappointment than pain. He's your brother, he said in a whisper, and I simply kept staring at the mess of records scattered on the floor. I thought of saying that I didn't have a brother, or that I didn't want a brother, or that I didn't want him as a brother. But I said nothing. My father sighed loudly and for a few seconds seemed to have been left with no air. Sit up straight, he ordered from the doorway, and I did, a little scared. Never before had my father hit me. And I don't know why—perhaps because of his faraway look, perhaps because I had it coming—I was sure that this would be the first time. My father finally entered the room and began to walk toward me through all the vinyl records on the floor, slowly, too slowly, as though he really didn't want to walk toward me, as though postponing the inevitable, until he finally stood beside me and reached out a hand and I prepared to receive a slap or a smack, but all I felt was something falling onto my chest.

It was the photo of the boy in the snow.

THAT NIGHT, THE NIGHT that he most should have shouted at me, my father did not. And I only listened to him in silence from the bed, though thinking all the while about the drowned boy in the lake, about the boy floating facedown by the dock, about that beautiful blond boy with the fearless face that I now, for perhaps the second time in my life, held in my hands.

My father, sitting on the edge of the bed, told me that he'd never met his brother Salomón. He told me that no one in the family knew many details of Salomón's life anymore, or of his death, since my grandparents rarely spoke about him. He told me that his brother had been born in 1935, sick, although it wasn't known sick with what, exactly. They said that Salomón was never able to walk very well, that he was never able to speak very well or that he never fully learned to speak, and that at one point he even stopped growing. That's why some people called him Chiqui—Little One—my father told me, because he stayed so little. Others called him Selim, which is Salomón in Arabic, and still others called him Shlomo, which is Salomón in Hebrew, his name in Hebrew, derived from the word shalom, which means peace. But my grandmother always called him Solly. The best doctors in the country, my father said, not knowing what else they could do for the boy, had recommended that my grandparents send him to a clinic in New York. A private clinic, he told me. A specialized clinic, where they could treat him better. He told me that in 1940, therefore, my grandmother and Salomón set sail from Puerto Barrios on a steamship called the *Antigua*, from the United Fruit Company's Caribbean fleet, for New York. Salomón was just five years old, and my grandmother, a young mother, only twenty-five, was taking him to New York on her own. My father didn't know why no one else had accompanied them, why my grandfather hadn't traveled with them. He told me that my grandmother had several times mentioned the name of that ship, that my grandmother had never forgotten the name of the ship, the *Antigua*, perhaps because there, on the sea, in the sea breeze, in the rocking waves of the sea, she'd

spent her final days with her firstborn son, with her
son Salomón, before leaving him forever in the private
clinic in New York. My father told me that the gray
snowy building in the photo, behind his brother, was
probably the clinic, but he couldn't be certain, and that
that photo in my hands had probably been taken by
my grandmother herself, in the summer of 1940, when
she said good-bye forever to her son in New York, but
that he couldn't be certain of that, either. He told me
that, sometime after having been admitted to the clinic
in New York—no one knew whether months or years
later—Salomón died of his illness. He was alone. With
no family at his side. Even though Aunt Lynda lived
there, close to him, in Atlantic City, in New Jersey, she
always insisted that she hadn't heard about his death
until much later. And they buried him in a common
cemetery, because nobody there, in that private clinic in
New York, knew that he was Jewish, and so they buried
him in a common cemetery, in a non-Jewish cemetery,
and with him they also buried his name. Nobody in
the family was named Salomón again. As if that name
was a living thing that had also been born sick and
traveled by boat and died in a private clinic in New
York. And nobody in the family spoke about Salomón
again, especially not my grandmother. He told me
that perhaps my grandmother never spoke about him
because her mother's sorrow was unfathomable, or
because silence was part of her mourning, or because

she never forgave herself for her son having died alone, for her son having been buried alone, with no loved ones, no family, no prayers, no Kaddish, no shivah, in a non-Jewish cemetery, in a random cemetery, perhaps in an anonymous grave, with no date and no name. He told me that in Hebrew there exists a word to describe a mother whose child has died. Maybe because that sorrow is so immense and so specific, it needs its own word. Sh'khol, it's called in Hebrew. My grandfather finally made a trip to New York in the forties or fifties to transfer Salomón's body to a Jewish cemetery. And that was the last my father knew of his brother, that was all he knew of his brother. He didn't know anything else. He didn't know what disease he'd died from, or what year he'd died in. He didn't even know the name of the Jewish cemetery in New York where he was buried. But at least, he told me, from the old photo I was still holding in my hands, from the photo in the snow, he did know his brother's face.

I AWOKE WITH MY NECK STIFF, my arms asleep, my back aching, my whole body in a knot in the hammock on the patio. I had a thick gray wool poncho over me. I supposed that someone, in the night, had led me to the hammock and covered me with that thick gray wool poncho. I still had the taste of burned water in my mouth. In the faint light of dawn, I managed to see that the candles were now colored stains on the patio floor, around the effigy. All that was left of the fire was a mound of coal and ash. The gourd bowl was empty at my feet. Also empty was Doña Ermelinda's chair. The decapitated turkey head had disappeared.

I closed my eyes and tried to remember something about the previous night. But my memories were disjointed images, chaotic, I didn't know whether real or dreamed or imagined. Doña Ermelinda blowing smoke in my face. Doña Ermelinda standing behind me, her bony hands rubbing my head. Doña Ermelinda plucking a white flower from the angel's trumpet and holding it tightly over my mouth and nose. Doña Ermelinda lighting only the black candles, telling me that one must never speak of the black candles. Doña Ermelinda laughing with Maximón. Doña Ermelinda dancing naked with Maximón in her arms. Doña Ermelinda telling me that I must have a child, that my life was senseless without a child. Doña Ermelinda holding a small hummingbird in her hand and rubbing it all over my body and telling me that it would help me have a child. Doña Ermelinda telling me or reminding me that the memory of a child is ennobled through music. Doña Ermelinda squatting down, urinating on the logs in the fire. Doña Ermelinda holding tobacco leaves to my abdomen and firmly pressing a wound on my abdomen and telling me there was something there, inside me, that was killing me. Doña Ermelinda and an old man in a straw hat watching me from up close while whispering in their language and then taking me to the hammock and covering me with the wool poncho. Doña Ermelinda making a noise like an owl and rocking me in the hammock and telling me not to forget my dreams, that it was important to remember my dreams the following morning, that in my dreams I would understand everything.

I took off the poncho and stood. But the dawn was chilly, so I put the poncho back over my shoulders and simply kept staring at the ground covered in ash and wax and dried blood. It struck me that I'd never found out which herbs or roots I had drunk the night before, that the old woman had given me the concoction in the gourd bowl without explaining anything to me, and that now it was better not to know. I looked up and understood that Doña Ermelinda was no longer inside her house. She'd probably set off before dawn, to the mountain, with her pack, to search for herbs. I didn't know if I should leave her some money, or if leaving her money might insult her. I took out a few bills and put them on the ground, beside the effigy, like an offering to Maximón.

I stepped off the patio, and the cool dawn air woke me up fully. I didn't feel exhausted, or sleep-deprived. On the contrary. I felt as though I were seeing everything for the first time, or for the last time. The deep red of a bougainvillea. A kingfisher perched on one branch of the araucaria, readying itself to fly off to the lake. The sparkling green of the mountain still drenched with rain. A lone small white cloud, as if forgotten or lost in the middle of the sky. In the distance, behind a wooden cayuco that was scarcely moving forward, the whole volcano, enveloped and protected in a light blanket of mist. But at the foot of the volcano, all along the water's shore, the abandoned lake houses now looked to me like the graves and crosses of a great cemetery, and the lake one single sarcophagus.

I adjusted the poncho slightly on my shoulders and walked toward the water. I wanted to dip my hands in to wash my face and neck, but a green crust of scum floated on the surface, so I simply kept contemplating the immensity of the lake, thinking about its stillness and its bounty, about its stoicism and its mythos, about the splendor that it once was. Here be dragons, I thought or perhaps whispered, looking down and recalling the phrase used by ancient cartographers who, standing on the shore of the unknown, at the end of the world, drew dragons on their maps. Then I looked up and noticed that the wooden cayuco was still approaching, though slowly. It took me a moment to realize that sitting in the old wooden vessel was a dark-skinned boy, thin, perhaps ten or twelve years old, and that he was rowing toward shore with a ping-pong paddle.

Morning, he said to me once he got close, smiling a bit timidly. It struck me, seeing the partially rotted red paddle in his hand, that, in fact, he'd approached relatively quickly. The tip of his cayuco wedged itself into the sludge on shore, right in front of me. Breakfast, mister? the boy asked, and I noticed that on the floor of the cayuco sat a Styrofoam ice chest and a school-type thermos covered in black plastic. He told me that he had tortillas with fresh cheese, tortillas with beans, tortillas with fried egg. I've got coffee, too, he said, still seated. He was wearing the sky blue jersey of I don't know what soccer team. How much for coffee? I asked, and the boy said three quetzals, five for tortillas. Well then, one coffee please, I said. The boy opened the ice chest, removed a little plastic cup, and set it down on the seat beside him. Then he unscrewed the top of the thermos and filled the little cup with coffee. Thank you very much, I said, taking the cup and giving him a ten-quetzal bill. And a tortilla for you, too, mister? he asked me, and I said no thank you as I took a sip. It was café de olla, fairly weak, but it was hot and acidic and the little cup felt good in my hands. Very tasty, I said, and the boy, still sitting and toying with the bill, smiled. Did you make the coffee and the tortillas yourself? I asked him. The boy shook his head emphatically, as though the question made no sense. My mother, he whispered. Of course, your mother, I repeated, and took another sip of coffee. I asked him if he went out every morning to sell breakfast around the lake. Almost, he said. And do you sell much? The boy looked down and took something from the floor of the cayuco that resembled an old cane made of rusted iron. Sometimes, he whispered. What about school? I asked him, but the boy simply shrugged. Don't you go to school? I asked. Sometimes, he said again, putting the bill in his pants pocket and taking out a few coins. No need, I said, keep the change. The boy scrunched his brow as though he didn't understand, as though the math didn't add up, but then he said thank you and got to his feet. Say, mister, he said suddenly, want to see what a big wave I can make? Sure, I replied, and then he flapped his free arm from side to side and let out a devilish little laugh. I smiled at him, imagining that this was the same joke he told all of his customers, every morning. He reached the iron cane out until he could drive it into the sludge onshore and then pushed back hard. The cayuco, slowly, released itself from the mud.

You're not from here, are you, mister? he asked me, sitting once more and rowing backward with his red paddle. I adjusted the poncho on my shoulders and took a hot sip of coffee. Sometimes, I said smiling. The boy smiled back, a big smile, two or three teeth missing.

I stood motionless onshore, wrapped tightly in the wool poncho, the steaming coffee in my hands, watching the boy move off toward the center of the lake with only the help of a small red paddle, his cayuco parting the surface, leaving behind a tiny wake. Suddenly the water before me seemed didn't seem so immense, or so stoic, or so green. I got a feeling in my chest that was a lot like euphoria, a euphoria that felt a lot like grief. And before I could think about it, before I even realized, I had already taken a couple of steps forward. I felt the icy water on my shoes, wetting my socks and pants. I felt the gentle waves on my shins, on my knees, rocking my entire body. I kept moving forward, entering the cayuco's wake, entering even farther, sinking a bit farther, and thinking the whole time about the boys who had left their lives in those same waters, about the boys who had entered the lake and gone down to the bottom and stayed there forever, about the boys who were now the children of nobody and the brothers of nobody, about the boys whose little shadows now walked with me, all of them together, and all of them kings of the lake, and all of them named Salomón.

About the Author

Eduardo Halfon moved from Guatemala to the United States at the age of ten and attended school in South Florida and North Carolina. The recipient of a Guggenheim Fellowship, Roger Caillois Prize, and José María de Pereda Prize for the Short Novel, he is the author of two previous novels published in English: *The Polish Boxer*, a *New York Times* Editors' Choice selection and finalist for the International Latino Book Award, and *Monastery*, longlisted for the Best Translated Book Award. Halfon currently lives in Nebraska and frequently travels to Guatemala.

The Translators

Lisa Dillman translates from Spanish and teaches in the Department of Spanish and Portuguese at Emory University in Atlanta, Georgia. She has translated numerous books by Spanish and Latin American writers including Andrés Barba, Christopher Domínguez Michael, Sabina Berman, and Yuri Herrera. Her translation of Herrera's *Signs Preceding the End of the World* received the Best Translated Book Award.

Daniel Hahn is a writer, editor, and translator with some fifty books to his name. His translations from Portuguese, Spanish, and French include fiction from Europe, Africa, and the Americas and nonfiction by writers ranging from Portuguese Nobel laureate José Saramago to Brazilian footballer Pelé. He is also the editor of the new *Oxford Companion to Children's Literature*. He lives in Lewes, England.

BELLEVUE LITERARY PRESS is devoted to publishing literary fiction and nonfiction at the intersection of the arts and sciences because we believe that science and the humanities are natural companions for understanding the human experience. With each book we publish, our goal is to foster a rich, interdisciplinary dialogue that will forge new tools for thinking and engaging with the world.

To support our press and its mission, and for our full catalogue of published titles, please visit us at blpress.org.

BELLEVUE LITERARY PRESS
New York